About the

Alan Gorevan is an award-winning writer and intellectual property attorney. He lives in Dublin. Visit his website at www.alangorevan.com

By Alan Gorevan

NOVELS:
Out of Nowhere

NOVELLAS:
The Forbidden Room
The Hostage
Hit and Run

SHORT STORY COLLECTION:
Dark Tales

The Thriller Collection

The Forbidden Room
The Hostage
Hit and Run

Alan Gorevan

Copyright © 2020 by Alan Gorevan

All rights reserved

No part of this book may be reproduced, stored in a retrieval system or transmitted by any means without the written permission of the author.

This book is a work of fiction. People, places, events and situations are the product of the author's imagination. Any resemblance to actual persons, living or dead, or historical events, is purely coincidental.

ISBN: 9798662649897

THE FORBIDDEN ROOM

CHAPTER ONE

Caroline Doherty sat in her little Peugeot, staring out the side window at the hills of west Cork. The air in the car was icy, but not as cold as outside. She gripped her phone, hoping the device would pick up a signal for the first time in half an hour.

This remote corner of Ireland was famous for its rugged beauty. Its hills, valleys and peninsulas were spectacular, not to mention its jagged cliffs towering over the Atlantic Ocean.

Caroline and her boyfriend, Jason Murphy, were headed for The Cliff View Guest House, located on the Beara Peninsula in the extreme south-west of the country. Evening was falling and the hotel was still some distance away. They were in a hilly area. Nothing but grass and rock all around them.

It was a terrible place for a car to break down.

As far as Caroline could tell, the nearest town was ten or fifteen miles away. Getting there would demand a long, dangerous walk. As well as being twisty, the road ahead was narrow and, of course, had no footpath.

The road behind them was equally bad. She couldn't imagine walking back to the petrol station they'd stopped at a few miles earlier. Out here, each mile felt like ten.

The late February light was beginning to fade. If they were walking on the road and a car came along, they'd be almost invisible. Jason was wearing a puffy black coat and dark jeans. Caroline's jeans and olive-coloured jacket were almost as dark. Her blonde hair was the only thing that might be visible in the gloom. Still, she figured that a driver was more likely to knock them down than give them a lift.

The road had clearly been cut out of the hillside, and there was not an inch to spare on either side. A rocky cliff rose up on the right side while, on the left, a hill of gorse fell away sharply. Rocky hills filled the middle distance.

Caroline opened the car door. At once, she felt the pounding of the rain. She opened her umbrella and walked over to Jason, who was still fiddling with the engine. Caroline was certain he had no more idea than she did about what was wrong with it. He insisted on trying to fix the thing anyway.

"Any luck?" Caroline shouted to be heard over the rain.

"Not yet."

Valentine's Day was meant to be romantic. A weekend break in the wilderness. Though they were both from Cork City, Caroline had taken frequent trips into the wilderness of West Cork when she was growing up. This place was a different world.

Largely unspoilt, it possessed a rough beauty that Jason didn't seem to appreciate. He was always more interested in staying in the city, or even going to Dublin, rather than exploring his own county's wild side.

"Can you shine a light here?" Jason shouted. He was bent over the engine, his face almost touching it.

Caroline turned on the torch on her phone and pointed it where Jason's hands were making a fumbling, uncertain exploration. It reminded her of the first time he'd tried to unhook her bra.

"It'll be dark soon," Caroline said.

"Why do you think I want a light?"

"I mean, we need to do something."

Jason straightened up and turned to her. His long black hair was plastered to his face and neck. His features, normally so chiselled and handsome, twisted into a sneer.

"What do you want me to do? I'm trying to start the fucking car."

Caroline flinched. During their six months together, she had rarely seen him angry. He hadn't wanted to come here, she knew. He'd only agreed to please her. But she'd been sure he'd start to enjoy himself once he arrived. She couldn't have known the car would cut out in the middle of nowhere.

"Look," she said, "I can't get a signal. You can't fix the car. We should try walking."

Jason looked around.

"On these roads?"

"I know, but we can't stay here. We have to try something," Caroline said. "We have to go somewhere."

"Just let me fix the car, will you?"

"You've been at it for ten minutes."

"If you weren't nagging me, I'd be finished by now."

Nagging.

The word slapped her across the face. So she was a nag now. Her first serious boyfriend had said it. Jason turned his attention to the engine again, not seeming to notice how much his words had hurt her.

Caroline turned off the torch app.

"Hey," Jason said, but she ignored him, and walked towards the back of the Peugeot. She didn't want to sit in the car. It was stopped in the middle of the road, blocking the lane. She imagined another car coming along and smashing into them. It was unlikely – traffic out here was infrequent – but her stomach churned with dread all the same.

She went and got the red warning triangle from the car's boot. She walked forty paces from the back of the car and set the triangle down on the tarmac. The only reason she hadn't put it out earlier was that Jason had seemed so confident he'd have the car running again in no time.

Just a second – that was the phrase he'd used, after the car cut out.

Caroline shook her head, wondering why she had listened. Jason played bass guitar in a rock band. He hadn't a mechanical bone in his body.

Just a second could mean *all night*.

As she was walking back towards the car, a gust of wind got under the umbrella and tore it from her hands. She let out a shout of surprise, and watched the umbrella fly away, over the side of the road and down the hill. She hurried over and looked down after it. An almost vertical drop greeted her. The ground levelled off far below, maybe eighty feet down. Nothing but gorse and rock and yellow heather. And – what was that?

Caroline squinted, shielding her eyes from the rain.

Was that…?

A flash of light on the road distracted her. She turned to see headlights approaching.

"Someone's coming," she shouted.

Caroline had never been so happy at the sight of a stranger's car. She'd started to get worried. After all, it was dark and stormy, and they were broken down, with no way to contact anyone. She jogged back to the Peugeot.

"What did you say?"

She grabbed Jason by the arm. "I said, someone's coming."

He straightened up. "I've nearly got it figured out," he said. "I think what we have here is a bad actuator."

"Never mind that. There's a car coming."

Ignoring Jason's scowl, she turned on her phone's torch function again and went around the side of the Peugeot. Standing in the middle of the other lane, she waved her hands in the air. The car was coming from the direction they had come. Maybe they could get a lift to The Cliff View Guest House.

The headlights of the oncoming car grew larger.

It didn't slow.

"Can they see us?" Caroline asked. She waved her phone higher in the air, hoping the light would be obvious.

The car was nearly upon them, and its roaring engine made Caroline's chest tighten. She waved her arms and called out, "Hey. Hey."

Jason straightened up and looked at the approaching car. His eyes widened.

"It's not stopping," he said. "Get out of the way."

CHAPTER TWO

Liam McGlynn's pale fingers shook as he gripped the steering wheel. The teenager was driving too fast. The truth was, he shouldn't have been driving at all – not in his state, and not in this weather.

Liam had driven halfway to his girlfriend, Emily's, house before he changed his mind and pulled in at the side of the road. He stopped there, intending to give himself a little time to think things over, but instead his eyes welled up with tears, and he sobbed like a child.

He wanted to get away from there. To be far away, with Emily by his side. But involving her in this was selfish. Liam had no money. He had nothing. Asking Emily to go away with him would have been asking her to give up any chance of a decent life. Liam didn't want that.

So he'd wiped his eyes with the sleeve of his hoodie, turned the Range Rover around and started to drive back home. He didn't want to do that, but what other option was there? No one was going to help him. No one cared.

As he approached the local petrol station, Liam saw an unfamiliar grey car at the pump. A seven-year old Peugeot 5008. Diesel. Manual transmission. It was pointed west, so he figured the driver was heading towards Liam's house.

He pulled in at the side of the forecourt and watched a couple get out of the car and head into the shop. They looked to be in their twenties. A skinny guy with long black hair, curled like it belonged to an 80s rock star, and a blonde woman, just as thin. They both wore puffy jackets and tight jeans. They looked like relatively normal people.

Liam got an idea.

He stepped out of the Range Rover. Crouching low, he hurried over to the Peugeot and grabbed a handful of sandy gravel from the ground. Liam knew engines. With a mechanic for a father, they had been a part of his life since he was born. He figured his idea might work.

He opened the fuel cap and shoved the gravel into the tank.

A second handful, then a third.

What he was planning was dangerous – and not just for him – but he could think of no other way out.

Liam glanced inside the shop. The woman was paying for her purchases. He closed the cap and, keeping low, jogged back to the Range Rover. When the couple emerged from the shop, he lowered himself in his seat so they wouldn't see him.

They probably wouldn't have observed him anyway. They were so absorbed in each other, talking and laughing. It was like the way he and Emily were, during their rare moments together.

Liam heard the couple drive off. He was relieved that their car was able to start. If it hadn't, then his plan would have failed. He rose in his seat, his heart thumping like crazy. Too shaky to drive.

It was fifteen minutes before he was calm enough to follow.

There was no sign of them on the road. He wondered if the gravel would do the job. It ought to, but when? The road ahead was empty.

Had he put enough gravel in?

What if it didn't work?

His stomach churned with anxiety, and he felt that he was going to be sick.

But when he rounded the next corner, he saw them. Dead ahead, the Peugeot's hazard lights were flashing. He drove through the red warning triangle almost before he registered its presence.

Despite the cold, his hands were slick with sweat. He wiped them on his hoodie, one after the other. The lady stood in his path, waving her arms.

I can't stop, Liam thought. *No way.*

He hit the accelerator.

CHAPTER THREE

The car veered into the wrong lane, hurtling towards Caroline. Its headlights were huge, blinding. She was still waving her hands in the air when she realised that it was going to hit her. To smash right into her without stopping.

She now saw that it was a huge, black SUV, the perfect vehicle for this terrain. The roar of its engine filled Caroline's ears. It was moving too fast, almost upon her. The driver pressed on the horn but didn't slow.

Caroline turned, trying to get out of the path of the danger, but her movements seemed sluggish. Her chest felt tight. This must be how a deer felt when it was blinded by a car.

I'll never make it, Caroline thought. *I'm going to die.*

The observation was terrifying, but at the same time, it felt strangely detached. Suddenly she felt light-headed. Caroline knew she was the one who was in danger, but it was as if she was watching someone else struggle to get to safety.

Then Jason grabbed her.

He pulled her towards him. Even as she was moving towards him, it was with excruciating slowness.

The car was almost upon her. She could smell its fumes.

Caroline squeezed her eyes shut and braced for the impact.

She felt heard the roar of the SUV's engine, felt its vibration in her chest, and then the vehicle shot past.

Caroline and Jason fell to the ground next to the Peugeot's front bumper. Jason hit the tarmac first, his head smashing against the ground, and Caroline fell on top of him, his body cushioning her fall. Jason grunted as the air was squeezed out of his lungs.

Caroline's heart was hammering in her chest.

She was alive.

"Are you okay?" she said.

"Yeah." Jason exhaled slowly. "You?"

"I think so."

Breathing hard, she disentangled herself from him. They staggered to their feet. The SUV disappeared out of sight around the corner. Jason came and stood next to Caroline.

"Maniac," he shouted.

Caroline shook her head. "What was that about?"

"They were going to drive straight into you."

Caroline shuddered. Her legs were weak as jelly. The rain continued to hammer down hard. "I don't understand how someone could act like that."

"Did you see the driver?"

"No. Not with those headlights in my eyes. I couldn't see a thing."

Jason glanced at the darkening sky. "I guess we shouldn't stand around here."

"Now you agree that we should walk?"

"Do you want an argument?"

"No," Caroline said.

"Your hands are cut," Jason said.

Caroline nodded impatiently. "You know, I saw something, before that car came." She walked to the edge of the road and looked down the steep hillside. Jason followed her.

"What?" he said. "I don't see anything."

Caroline shivered. Both of them were drenched to the skin. The puffy jacket she wore was sold as "water resistant" but that was a lie. The rain had started soaking into it as soon as the first drop hit the fabric. Her eyes scanned the land below.

Caroline pointed and said, "Look down there."

"At the bottom?"

"Yeah. See that grey line? Is that a road?"

Jason squinted for a long time. "It's hard to tell, with those bushes in the way. No," he said at last. "I don't think so."

"I think it is."

"Why did you ask me then?"

She ignored him. "There might be a house," Caroline said. "It looks like a one-lane road. Private property."

Jason looked sceptical. "Even if it is, how are we meant to get there? We might have to drive miles to find the way to it. And the car is still dead."

"A straight line is the shortest distance between two points," Caroline said. Though the hillside was very steep, Caroline figured they could scramble down it if they were careful. She played basketball once a week and went to the gym at least twice. She wasn't afraid of a little exertion.

"Are you sure?" Jason asked. "I don't want you slipping and breaking your neck."

"Like you say, if we go the long way around, it could take hours. If we go this way, it might take a couple of minutes. Let's go."

Jason looked reluctant, probably because the plan wasn't his. He'd probably have preferred to continue tinkering with the Peugeot's engine.

"Hold on."

He ran back to the car. Opening the back door, he took out their overnight bags, then jogged back over.

He said, "Better to bring them, right?"

"Sure. Can you help me down?"

Jason placed their bags at his feet and held onto Caroline's hand as she lowered herself from the side of the road to the grassy slope below, a gap of three or four feet.

Jason jumped down next to her, but he lost his balance, got caught in the two overnight bags, and rolled into some bright yellow heather. He got to his feet, swearing loudly.

"Watch out," Caroline said.

"Fuck off."

Maybe it was the fact that she had nearly died, but Caroline felt a touch of giddiness. Relief at being alive. She grabbed Jason's neck, pulled his face close to hers, and kissed his cheek.

"I love you," she said.

Jason stared at her. Neither of them had said those words. And just a few minutes ago, Caroline had felt like killing him.

But whatever.

She was *alive*. That was worth celebrating.

Smiling to herself, she set off down the slope, being careful to keep her balance as she stepped on rock and mud. Heather brushed against her legs. The valley floor was not a long way down, but she hated even moderate heights.

Over the rain, Jason shouted, "Someone should build a slide here."

Caroline smiled. "That would be fun."

"Did you recognise the SUV?"

"No. Why would I?"

Jason said, "I think I saw one like that at the place where we stopped."

Caroline thought back to the petrol station where they bought a snack. She had been completely focused on selecting chocolate bars while Jason chose a packet of crisps. Sweet versus savoury. They never agreed on anything. She didn't remember any other customers.

Caroline shrugged, "I don't know. Maybe."

They continued down. After a minute, Caroline reached the place where her umbrella had landed after being blown out of her hands. It was caught up in more heather. She worked it free and closed the umbrella. There was no point trying to shield herself from the rain now. They were as wet as they could get, and Caroline needed both hands to keep her balance. She stuffed the umbrella into the pocket of her jacket and continued on her way.

They finally reached the bottom of the hill. A rough road stretched out in both directions.

Caroline nodded to the left. "I think it's that way."

"How do you know?"

"A feeling."

She didn't wait for a reply, just started walking. The trail curved around a rocky outcrop and led downwards.

"We're probably going the wrong way," Jason grumbled.

The road went on much longer than Caroline expected. They walked for ten minutes before a huge yew tree appeared ahead of them.

"Do you hear that?" Jason said.

"What?"

He said, "Sounds like the sea."

"I don't hear anything." *Except rain,* Caroline thought.

"You're not a musician. Your ears aren't trained like mine."

Caroline walked around the yew tree.

Standing in front of her was a large, ramshackle bungalow, its stonework covered in peeling white paint.

Lights blazed in its windows.

CHAPTER FOUR

In the sprawling garage, Liam McGlynn stepped out of the Range Rover. He closed the door and walked to the house, zipping up his hoodie, and then his jacket, to protect himself from the bitter cold.

It was a miracle he hadn't crashed on the way home as he wasn't in control of himself. He kept thinking back to earlier in the day, remembering the sound of the mirror breaking.

Stop it.

There was a way out.

The couple in the Peugeot had broken down at a good place, but that didn't mean they'd find the house. Liam hoped they would, though. There was nothing else nearby.

The panicked feeling he'd had since lunchtime had only grown worse as the Range Rover bounced along the road to the house. Terror snaked up Liam's throat as he wondered what Doreen and Steve would do.

For Liam, it had always been *Doreen and Steve*, never *Mum and Dad*. They didn't let him use those words. Only Frank had been allowed to say that.

What if they discovered the trick he'd pulled with the couple? They were already at his throat.

Liam was starting to regret not going to Emily's house as he had planned. Perhaps the two of them didn't need to run away. Maybe her parents would shelter him. Liam could have explained things – could have *tried*, anyway. Emily was sympathetic.

Some people shouldn't be allowed to be parents.

She said that after Liam told her about the goldfish.

Doreen had purchased them when Liam and Frank were eight. One fish ate the other while the boys were at school. Liam had cried when he found out – because it was his fish that had been eaten. Doreen said it didn't matter. His fish was only a poor copy of its brother.

"Like you," she added.

Nearly a decade later, Liam still felt a chill when he remembered the way Doreen looked at him as she said it.

He walked around the back of the bungalow, rubbing his hands together as he went.

Steve stood outside the door with a cigarette in his hand. He gave Liam a cool stare as his son approached. Liam stopped, well away from him, and put his hands in his pockets.

"Where did you go?" Steve said.

"For a drive."

"Who'd you talk to?"

Liam shook his head. "Nobody."

Liam pulled out the torch and smashed it as hard as he could into Steve's face. With a grunt, Steve released him and fell in a heap on the ground.

Liam ran towards the cliff before Steve could recover.

"I'm just saying, we don't know who lives here."

"Then let's find out."

She left Jason standing there and walked towards the house. A large garage stood to the side of the bungalow. Its double doors were closed.

Caroline made her way up to the door. It was solid wood. No glass in it, so she couldn't see inside. No sign of a doorbell. She knocked – knocked hard, to be heard over the rain. As her knuckles rapped on the wood, Caroline heard voices inside. They fell silent as soon as she knocked.

She glanced at Jason, as he caught up with her on the doorstep.

"Did you hear that?"

Jason nodded. "Let's go," he said. "I don't like this."

"We can't go now. They heard us."

"I don't want to walk in on… you know."

Jason hated family disagreements, even mild ones. His parents had split up when he was thirteen. Jason rented his own flat the day he turned eighteen and hadn't spoken to his family in the seven years since.

Caroline touched his arm.

"We'll ask to use their phone. We'll call for help. That's it. It'll take ten minutes. Then we can get on with our weekend."

Jason looked at his watch. "It's five o'clock now. I'm not feeling very romantic."

"Neither am I," Caroline said, "but I planned this whole weekend for you."

Jason sighed. "Fine."

Caroline tried to cheer herself up. The Cliff View Guest House was waiting for them. It would have sparkling wine and a bowl of fruit ready at check-in, plus a vase of fresh flowers in the bedroom. She had chosen a room with a breath-taking view of the Atlantic, nothing but waves as far as the eye could see, though she was getting a preview of that vista now, and the sea looked rough.

A hiking tour of the cliffs was arranged for the following morning. She'd thought it would be something to look forward to, after spending this evening enjoying local seafood and relaxing in the bar.

Booking the weekend had made Caroline feel like an adult. At twenty-seven, she considered herself a late bloomer. She had never gone away with a boyfriend before, had never even had a serious boyfriend before. Jason seemed special.

Now, as she watched a vein bulge in Jason's forehead, Caroline wasn't so sure about that.

He said, "Jesus, are these bastards going to open up or not?"

He pounded his fist against the door.

"Hello? Anyone home?"

Caroline heard footsteps approaching.

CHAPTER SIX

Steve McGlynn staggered towards the house, his hands out in front of him as if he was blind, though he wasn't. He was just dazed.

Shielding his eyes from the rain, he glanced back at the path that ran along the cliff face. Liam had already vanished into the darkness.

"You'll be back," he shouted.

Steve touched the side of his head, beside his eyebrow. His fingers came away bloody. He wondered how bad the wound was. It hurt like a bitch. For a second, he'd thought the little prick was going to kill him.

Kill *him.*

After everything Steve had done for him.

The back door of the house swung open and Doreen poked her head out. Steve's wife hadn't changed much since they met nearly thirty years earlier. She'd been a top-of-the-class veterinary student. He'd been an apprentice mechanic. Steve knew the moment he saw her that there was something special about Doreen. He hadn't changed his mind about that.

When angry, she still gave him that look, her deep-set eyes burning darkly, but her face otherwise blank.

She took in at a glance his injury and the fact that he was alone.

"Where's Liam?" Doreen asked.

Still dizzy, Frank reached out and grabbed the handrail next to the door. Doreen took his arm and helped him into the kitchen, closing the door behind her.

"Gone," Steve said. "Ran off to find Barney, once he smashed me in the face."

Doreen helped him to a chair at the kitchen table and said, "We're not going to let him away with it."

Steve shook his head. "I don't intend to. But he's strong as a horse, that boy." His eyes narrowed. "What exactly should we do?"

Doreen had always been the one with a plan. When they met, she'd been so determined to become a vet. Of course, she hadn't been allowed to finish her degree after her dean found out she'd been the one killing the squirrels on campus. Hard to understand the fuss. Damn things were only rodents. Maybe Doreen shouldn't have hung them around the campus from tree branches though.

She said, "We have to punish him. Did he talk to anyone?"

"I don't think so."

"If he opens his big mouth, who knows what he might say?"

Steve scowled. "We didn't do anything wrong. He's the one who—"

Someone knocked on the front door. The sound was so unfamiliar, it took Steve a moment to recognise the sound.

"Did you hear that?" he said.

Doreen opened the door to the hall.

Someone pounded on the door again. A man's voice. "Hello? Anyone home?"

Steve's eyes widened. "Oh shit," he said. "They're here to arrest us."

"Shut up," Doreen hissed.

"Don't open the door," Steve said. "They'll go away."

"The lights are on."

"They'll go away," he repeated.

"We can't act suspicious. You go and get yourself tidied up," Doreen said.

"Don't," Steve said. "You'll make things worse."

But Doreen was already walking down the hall.

CHAPTER SEVEN

Caroline waited as the door opened to reveal a stout woman in her fifties. She wore an apron over a flowery blouse, and beige trousers. Curly, greying hair framed a round face, but something about her mouth reminded Caroline of a trout.

The woman kept her hand on the door, as if ready to slam it shut again if they gave her a reason.

Caroline's nostrils filled with the smell of baking. Something sweet and fruity. Her stomach rumbled.

Jesus, are these bastards going to open up or not?

Jason's words rang in her ears. Caroline couldn't remember the last time she'd been so mortified. Why did he have to say such a thing?

"We're so sorry to bother you," Caroline said. She smiled at the lady. "Our car broke down on the road."

She pointed back the way they had come.

"Broke down?"

"We don't know what the problem is but—"

"Maybe a bad actuator," Jason interrupted.

The woman stared at their soaking clothes.

Caroline said, "We weren't able to call a mechanic. My phone couldn't find a signal. Could we use yours to call for help? We'd really appreciate it."

The woman seemed to think for a moment, then opened the door wide.

"You better come in," she said, stepping back.

Caroline smiled. "Thank you so much."

She wiped her feet on the welcome mat inside the door. The woman closed the door behind Jason. Narrow as it was, the hallway was warm, and for that Caroline was grateful. The dark blue walls were covered with framed photos of a family.

"This is a lovely house," Caroline said. It was only a white lie.

"Thank you," the woman said. "Follow me."

She had a stronger Cork accent than Caroline or Jason, maybe because they were from the city. This woman's accent was so strong, it turned *follow me* into a question, and had a musical, lilting quality.

Caroline glanced at the photos as she followed the woman down the hall. They showed the woman at various ages, always with a man and a boy. No, two boys. But one liked to lurk in the background.

"Sorry for dripping water on your floor," Caroline said.

"Don't worry about it."

That sounded like a question too.

The woman closed the door to a laundry room. Not the prettiest room in the house, Caroline guessed. She glimpsed a washer, a dryer, and a rack with keys on the wall. Of course, the woman wasn't expecting guests. How would Caroline have felt if two strangers turned up on her door without any warning and she had to let them in? She'd be wondering what to hide too.

The woman led them into a sprawling kitchen. It was even warmer in here, and the scent of baking was stronger. Caroline's mouth watered. If she had seen a photo of this room in a magazine, the kitchen would have been described as rustic. It had an old wood-burning stove, tins and glass jars everywhere. No sign of a microwave or anything else modern.

Through the window, Caroline could just about discern the movement of the ocean. The thought of its cold, dark water made her shiver.

A groan made Caroline whip around. There was another doorway on the other side of the kitchen.

"Don't worry," the woman said. She took off her apron and put it on a hook next to the oven. "That's only my husband. He slipped in the garden."

"Is he hurt?" Caroline asked. "I did a first aid course at work."

"He's fine. Don't worry. I'm Doreen McGlynn, by the way."

"I'm Caroline. This is Jason."

They shook hands. Doreen's grip was firm. There was a firmness in her blue eyes, too.

"Is it just you and your husband here?" Jason asked.

Doreen's eyes twinkled. "Oh no. We have the twins. Frank and Liam."

Caroline caught sight of a landline on the wall.

"Can we call somebody? I'm happy to pay you."

Doreen shook her head. "I wouldn't take your money, even if the phone worked. But the line is down."

"Pardon?" Jason said.

"The storm has knocked out the line. You can't phone anyone."

CHAPTER EIGHT

Caroline's disappointment must have registered on her face because Doreen reached out and squeezed her arm. Caroline didn't like strangers touching her, but she was too surprised to protest.

"It's okay," Doreen said. "The phone will be working again soon."

"You mean tonight?" Jason asked.

"Oh, no. The storm is getting worse. Look at that." Outside, the rain had turned to sleety snow. It slapped against the window, and began to pile up on the sill. "No one's going to be out fixing things tonight."

"Fuck," Jason said. "This is unbelievable."

Caroline shot him a look. "Jason."

"Excuse me," he said. "But fuck."

Doreen lumbered over to the window and closed the curtains.

Caroline pictured herself and Jason trudging back to the car, getting inside the ice-cold interior and freezing to death during the night – if they weren't rear-ended by another motorist first.

Jason said, "Is there no mobile phone signal around here?"

"It's always hopeless," Doreen said. "You have to go a few miles down the road to get a reliable signal."

Jason shook his head in disbelief. "How do you live here?"

"Well, it has its good points. There's the peace and quiet. And usually we're in communication with the world. Oh, my baking!"

Doreen opened the oven, and used a pair of mitts to remove a tart with rich golden-brown pastry. While she set it down on the worktop, Caroline closed the oven door.

"Thank you," Doreen said, giving her a smile.

"So," Caroline said. "There's no way to contact anyone tonight?"

"I'm afraid not," Doreen said, straightening up. "The good news is my husband's a mechanic. I'm sure he'd be happy to look at your car."

"Excellent," Jason said.

"But he can't do it tonight. Not in this weather, and not with the bang on the noggin he just got. But in the morning." Doreen glanced at Caroline again, then looked Jason up and down. "We have a spare room. You're welcome to stay the night with us."

"That's very kind, but we don't want to impose. You don't even know us."

"I don't think there's much of a choice. Look at you. You're drenched. And it's snowing now." Doreen leaned forward. "You'd die out there."

Jason ran a hand through his hair, a reliable indicator that he was frustrated.

"You're very kind," Caroline said. "I guess we'll have to take you up on that offer."

Doreen waved her hand. "Living in the countryside makes you practical. You do whatever you have to do."

Caroline heard footsteps. A moment later, the door to the kitchen opened and a man Doreen's age appeared. He was stout, a little more so than his wife, and had a kiwi-fruit haircut and a short, grey beard. He wore round glasses with golden frames.

Caroline stared at the gash on the side of his head.

She said, "Oh my god, I think you need stitches."

The man glanced at Doreen. She walked over and put her arm around him.

"Say hello to Caroline and Jason. Their car broke down on the road. I've said they can wait here till morning. This is my husband, Steve."

"That's rotten luck," Steve said, sounding genuinely upset.

Doreen led her husband to a chair at the kitchen table. He lowered himself into it slowly. When he put a finger to his head, Doreen slapped it away.

She said, "I'll fix up Steve's wound and then we'll see about getting you two warm and dry."

"Thank you so much," Caroline said. "There's no hurry."

Water was dripping from her hair down her face. Despite what she said, she could feel the cold and wet seeping into her bones. The woman was right. They wouldn't last long outdoors tonight.

CHAPTER NINE

Caroline began to feel her clothes drying off in the heat of the kitchen. Doreen had given her and Jason towels to dry their hair with, and that helped.

Steve sat at the kitchen table, with Jason next to him. Caroline hovered nearby, hoping to make herself useful, as Doreen cleaned out Steve's wound with a damp cloth.

"Looks like you need some TLC too," Doreen said, when she noticed Caroline's grazed palms.

"Sorry?"

"Tender loving care. You better rinse those cuts."

"Oh, right."

Caroline washed her hands under the cold tap. As she dabbed them dry with a few sheets of kitchen roll, she told Doreen how she had been forced to jump out of the path of the SUV.

Doreen dabbed antiseptic onto a tissue and patted Caroline's wounds. It stung. Caroline winced but didn't make a sound.

She shuddered at the thought of her lucky escape, how close she had come to being killed before she even turned thirty.

Blood dripped down Steve's face as his wife worked. He seemed calm, or else he was still dazed from his fall. Either way, he didn't protest.

Jason kept his eyes averted. Though he came across as a tough guy, Caroline knew he couldn't stomach the sight of blood. He didn't like to talk about it much, but Caroline had gathered, over their time together, that Jason's father was a violent drunk. Hence the broken marriage. And hence the broken bones that still gave Jason grief if he played bass guitar for too long at a time.

"There," Doreen said, finishing up. She dabbed the wound and admired her handiwork. "You sit down and have a rest."

Steve grunted as he got to his feet. He adjusted his glasses, then padded off towards the front of the house.

Doreen turned to Caroline.

"Now. What should we do with you two?"

CHAPTER TEN

Doreen left Jason and Caroline in the kitchen and went to make up the spare bedroom. Caroline had offered to help, but Doreen wouldn't hear of it, and Caroline could understand that. She might not want her guests to see the spare room yet, if it was a mess.

"Now don't touch my apple tart," Doreen said, waving a finger at them.

She clicked the door shut behind her.

"These people give me the creeps," Jason said. He jumped up from the kitchen table and walked in a circle around the room. "There's something wrong with them."

"Shut up. There's something wrong with *you*."

"I'm serious."

Caroline rolled her eyes. "Because they live in the countryside?"

"Yes," Jason said. He rubbed his eyes. "No. But living in the countryside doesn't help. It's not a point in their favour – I'll tell you that much."

"They're giving us a room for the night. They're taking us in."

"I wouldn't do that if I was them."

"Because you're so selfish."

Jason reversed his direction and began circling the room the opposite way.

"Exactly," he said. "Normal people are selfish."

"So you're saying this sweet couple has some sort of ulterior motive? That's why they offered to let us stay here?"

"Maybe."

"Like what?" Caroline said.

Jason shrugged. He stopped pacing and stood in front of the apple tart.

"I'm so hungry," he said.

"Oh my god." Caroline watched as Jason reached out. "Don't even think of touching that," she hissed.

"I want to try it."

"Don't."

Jason shot her a wolfish grin and thrust his index finger into the tart. He pulled it out straight away.

"Fuck!" he shouted. "It's hot."

Caroline hissed, "Of course, it is. Be quiet."

He put his finger in his mouth and sucked it.

"Jesus."

He went to the sink and put his finger under the cold-water tap. When he took it out from under the water, his finger looked as pink as a crab.

"Nice going," Caroline said.

"Tasty, though."

A gruff voice said, "What's going on?"

Steve was standing in the doorway.

"Sorry," Caroline said.

"What was that shouting?"

"I sat on my finger," Jason said.

"Sat on your finger?" Steve frowned.

"Sorry," Caroline said. "We'll keep it down. How are you feeling?"

"Fine. A little dizzy."

"Maybe you need to sit down?"

"Yeah. You're probably right."

Steve turned and left the room.

Caroline breathed a sigh of relief. Jason could be so goofy sometimes. The apple tart sat on the worktop, a big finger-hole in it.

"That's great," she said. "That's just great. They ask us not to do one thing, and you do it."

Jason grinned. "What are they going to do about it?"

CHAPTER ELEVEN

Fifteen minutes later, Doreen led Caroline and Jason down a hallway. The house had a weird layout with the kitchen at centre, the point where two hallways met. Doreen pushed open the door to the spare bedroom.

"I made up a bed for you and tidied the room a little."

"Thank you so much," Caroline said. She stepped inside and saw a double bed. Doreen had left some towels on top of the covers. A wardrobe stood on one side of the bed and a computer desk on the other.

Doreen said, "There's only one bed. Do you mind sharing?"

"Not a problem," Jason said.

Doreen took a pile of clothes off the desk and set it down on the bed.

"I found you some dry clothes. My old stuff for you, Caroline. Some of Frank's for you, Jason. That's our eldest son."

"Great," Jason said. "Because our bags are soaked through. We can't wear any of our spare clothes."

"Don't worry. I'll do the laundry tonight. Wash and dry all your clothes. In the meantime, I hope Frank's clothes fit you. The bathroom is at the end of the hall. You can have a shower and get warm."

Caroline smiled. She felt genuinely touched by the woman's kindness.

Doreen stepped back into the hallway.

"Get nice and warm and dry," she said. "Then come and we'll see about dinner. It'll be ready in half an hour. I hope you have a good appetite."

Caroline smiled. "Oh yes."

"You didn't spoil it?"

"Nope," Jason said.

"Good. Make yourselves at home."

Caroline said, "Again, thank you so much."

She followed Doreen out to the hallway. Doreen smiled and turned to go back towards the kitchen. Caroline walked down the hall, stopped at the next door, and reached for the handle.

"Not that room!" Doreen shouted.

Caroline pulled her hand back in shock. The woman was glaring at her.

"I'm sorry. I—"

"The bathroom is at the end of the hall. The end!"

"Sorry. I don't know what I was thinking."

Caroline felt like a school pupil being scolded by a belligerent teacher. Jason appeared in the doorway of the spare room, a confused look on his face. Doreen walked over to Caroline.

"It's okay," Doreen said. "But that's Frank's room. Don't go in there. He's very private, very particular about his personal space. Enjoy the rest of the house. Relax in the kitchen or the sitting room. Whatever you like. But not Frank's room."

"I'm so sorry," Caroline said.

"The bathroom is at the end of the hall. Okay?"

"Absolutely. Got it. We won't bother Frank." Caroline gave a nervous laugh. She stopped smiling when Doreen didn't smile back. "Where *are* your sons?"

"Oh, they're around somewhere."

"Will they be joining us for dinner?"

"I'm sure they will. Liam will, at least. I better let you get cleaned up."

Doreen turned and walked away.

Caroline felt shocked by Doreen's reaction. She followed Jason into the spare room.

"Was that weird or what?" he said.

Caroline was breathing too hard to reply for a moment. Her body reacted to emotional stress as if it was physical exercise. "A bit," she finally managed to say.

Jason was examining the spare clothes Doreen had left him.

"Not my style," he said, looking at the woolly cream-coloured jumper. He unfolded the pale blue jeans. "Not my style."

"I'll have a shower," Caroline said, because she thought if she didn't get a break from Jason, she'd slap him.

Doreen had left her a pair of baggy jeans, a T-shirt and a warm jumper. They were far too big, but Caroline didn't mind, as long as she got into something dry. There were socks too, but no underwear.

"Are we going commando?" Jason said.

"I guess. I'm drenched all the way through."

Jason nodded thoughtfully and went over to the window. He pulled open the curtains and looked out into the darkness of the evening. Sleety snow was still falling.

He said, "Why do I feel creeped out?"

"How would I know? Because you're an oversensitive musician?"

"Let's just get out of here as fast as we can, okay?"

Caroline was surprised when Jason turned, and she saw his face. He wasn't goofing around like he had been in the kitchen.

"Okay," she said. "Shower, eat, sleep. Leave first thing in the morning."

Jason nodded. "Sounds like a plan. Though I'd still prefer to leave right now."

"Go ahead."

He smiled. "Maybe I will."

CHAPTER TWELVE

Liam McGlynn jogged along the cliff path, hood up, gloves on, his chest burning. The sleet had stopped for the moment, but an icy wind continued to gust.

The slate grey sea churned a hundred and fifty feet below. It was at times like this that the immensity of the ocean impressed itself upon Liam. Salty sea air filled his senses.

The path was only a few paces from the cliff edge. Sometimes Liam was tempted to hurl himself over the edge. It would be a brutal fall. The cliffs were rocky and you could easily hit the cliffside as you fell. Then at the bottom, your body would be broken on the jagged rocks where the waves crashed.

No, he had a job to do.

He had to find Barney. No one else cared about the golden retriever, but Liam loved that dog. Barney was out here somewhere, alone. Liam couldn't stand the thought.

Moving quickly, he urged himself down the path. He thought of Emily. Liam could hardly believe he'd found a girl who wanted to spend time with him, someone who cared. But he had. Emily and Barney. The only things in the world that he cared about.

Tonight was no ordinary night. He'd get away from this hellhole. Tonight. He promised himself he would, just as soon as Barney was safe.

The thundering roar of the waves was fantastic. Liam wondered if he'd be able to hear Barney if he barked. He continued jogging for another ten minutes but found no sign of the dog.

What if Barney had returned to the house?

It seemed likely, given the weather.

Liam decided to turn back. But before he did, he shouted his dog's name. The wind tore his voice away. He waited but there was no response, no sign of Barney anywhere.

CHAPTER THIRTEEN

Caroline left Jason pondering his fashion choices in the bedroom. She took the towels and Doreen's spare clothes and stepped into the hallway.

Six doors opened onto the hall. One led back to the kitchen. There was the guest room that she and Jason had been assigned, and another door stood opposite. It was slightly ajar, and Caroline glimpsed a bedroom. The décor looked mature, so she figured the room belonged to Doreen and Steve.

She started down the hall, passing Frank's room on the way – the room she was forbidden to enter. She wondered why Frank was so private. What did he do in there? There was no sound from within, so Caroline thought Frank must not be home.

A fifth door faced Frank's room. Maybe this one belonged to the other son, Liam. No sound from that room either.

At the end of the hall was the sixth and final door. The bathroom.

Caroline stepped inside. The room was bigger than she expected, nothing like the cramped one she had in her own apartment. Everything here was blue, from the tiles on the walls to the ceramic sink, and even the toilet bowl. It looked weird and somehow dated. But it seemed clean – except for a spatter of blood on the mirror.

Steve must have come here to check his wound.

The bathroom was a little cooler than the rest of the house.

The window had no blind, but its glass was heavily frosted, so no one could see in – at least, they could see nothing more than a blur – which was a relief, considering that she was on the ground floor.

She closed the door behind her and reached down to lock it, only to find that there was no key in the lock. There was no bolt either, no way to secure the door.

As far as Caroline was concerned, a lock was the number one thing you needed in a bathroom. Maybe they didn't have many guests out here, but still, four people lived in the house. How could they not want to lock the door?

"Okay," she said.

It was what it was.

She should just get on with things.

Be fast.

She used the toilet quickly, watching the door the whole time, and listening for the sound of someone coming. Nothing, except the sound of the wind outside.

She set down Doreen's spare clothes on top of a small chest of drawers, then stripped. She piled her own wet clothes on the floor.

Now that she was naked, she felt vulnerable. She opened the glass doors of the shower stall and peered at the electric shower. The machine looked simple enough, not like the baffling devices in most hotels. Reaching in, she turned on the water, and adjusted the temperature until it was as hot as she could stand. Then she stepped under the water and closed the doors behind her.

Relief washed over her and she began to warm up under the falling water. There was shampoo and shower gel on the shelf in the shower stall. They had a pleasant floral scent, and Caroline enjoyed the luxurious feeling the hot shower gave her.

She decided to leave Doreen and Steve some money as compensation for using their bathroom supplies. Caroline didn't have a lot of cash, but she wasn't stingy with what she did have, and she felt guilty for imposing on them – especially if Steve was going to help them tow the Peugeot in the morning.

She turned off the water and stepped onto the towel on the floor.

The air felt different. Thinner. Caroline looked around, confused.

The door to the hall stood open an inch.

Caroline stared at it. She had shut the door. Even though she hadn't been able to lock it, she'd shut it firmly. She didn't see how it could have opened by itself. Had someone come into the bathroom while she had been showering? While she had her eyes closed?

No.

Surely not.

She crossed the room quickly and closed the door. She pulled the handle to see if it opened easily, but it didn't.

Maybe Jason was messing with her? He could be annoying. But would he be this mean?

Caroline noticed that the pile of wet clothes was gone. Only a small puddle of water remained.

Someone *had* been in the room.

She went over to the pile of clothes she had set down on the chest of drawers, intending to get dressed as quickly as possible.

Someone had placed a pair of lacy underwear on top of the pile.

CHAPTER FOURTEEN

Once she had dressed, Caroline hurried down the corridor to the bedroom. Doreen's old jeans were so loose at the waist, Caroline had to hold them up as she walked.

She had left the underwear in the bathroom. She wasn't going to wear them. For one thing, they belonged to someone else, or they had at one time. The thought of wearing another woman's panties disgusted her. For another thing, she was livid at their appearance in the room.

How dare someone invade her privacy like that?

She pushed open the door to the spare bedroom and stepped inside.

"You're never going to believe this…" Caroline said, but the room was empty. Where was Jason?

She ducked back into the hall, then made her way to the kitchen. Doreen was standing at the oven. A teenage boy stood next to the door to the back garden. He had messy brown hair and skin that was pale as milk. He wore a fluffy black hoodie over a purple T-shirt, plus pale jeans and runners. The boy looked nervous.

Caroline remember being that age. Sometimes she wondered how she'd ever got through it. And how people had tolerated her.

Coming into the room, she had fully intended to demand to know who came into the bathroom while she was showering. The sight of the boy's face changed her mind. He looked like he'd just been slapped across the face with a fish. Was it him? Did he put the underwear in the room as some kind of joke? Or maybe Doreen was the one who had entered the bathroom, and she was just trying to be helpful.

Caroline decided to hold off on making any accusations.

"This is my son, Liam," Doreen said.

Holding the jeans with one hand, to keep them from falling down, Caroline went over and held out the other out to Liam. He swallowed – she saw his Adam's apple move – and then gave her a limp hand. Caroline took it and did all the shaking.

"Nice to meet you."

The boy muttered something she didn't catch.

Caroline said, "Where's Jason?"

"Outside, smoking with Steve." Doreen shook her head. "Sometimes, I really don't understand men."

Caroline nodded. "It's a filthy habit."

"I smoke too," Doreen said. "But not outside during a blizzard."

"Oh, well," Caroline said, "each to their own."

The top half of the back door was glass, covered by a blind. Caroline lifted it and peered into the darkness. It was fully dark now and she couldn't see anything.

She sighed.

"I suppose your husband definitely wouldn't be able to tow my car tonight?"

"I don't think so. He's still woozy. He really shouldn't. And don't worry, there'll be no traffic on the road tonight. No one's going to hit your car."

"That's what I'm worried about."

"No need," Doreen said. "I promise."

Caroline turned to Liam. "Do you drive?"

"I, uh—"

"He's only seventeen," Doreen said. "He's still learning. Don't you worry. Everything is going to be fine." She took a step closer to Caroline and pinched her cheek. "You're so… *conscientious*."

Caroline forced a laugh, but the pinch hurt.

"Casserole's ready," Doreen said. "Let's eat. If we can round up the men."

CHAPTER FIFTEEN

Steve and Jason walked around the bungalow while they smoked. Jason hadn't had a cigarette since Christmas, and it felt so good.

He had decided against a shower. While Caroline was in the bathroom, Jason had changed out of his wet clothes and put on Frank's dry ones. When he went to the kitchen, Steve was getting a beer from the fridge. Would have been rude to refuse. And cigarettes went so well with beer.

From the back, he could see how large the house was. It looked like it had been added to over the years, giving the building a ramshackle quality.

"The previous owner was a builder," Steve said, pointing his cigarette at the house as they walked.

Not a good one, Jason thought, but he said nothing.

His hands were numb, but he savoured the nicotine rush.

"What do you do out here?" Jason said.

Steve broke out in a fit of coughing. "Enjoy the peace," he said. "We like to keep to ourselves most of the time. I do auto repairs. Doreen is a natural born baker. Sells her cooking at a farmer's market and online."

"That must be tough when the internet isn't working."

"It works most days."

There was no moon. Though Jason could sense the immensity of the ocean nearby, he could see little.

They walked around the side of the house, to where the garage stood.

"Are you going to show me your tow truck?" Jason said.

"Not right now." Steve threw his cigarette on the ground. "We better get back inside. I reckon dinner is ready."

"Just a quick look? I'm pretty curious. I always wanted to drive one of those things."

Jason heard the kitchen door open.

"Dinner," Doreen called.

Steve smiled in the darkness. "Let's go. You don't want to make her wait. She can be mean as hell."

CHAPTER SIXTEEN

Doreen removed the casserole from the oven. She instructed everyone to sit down at the table while she plated the meal.

Liam helped, bringing plates to the table. He was relieved Caroline and Jason had found the house. Their presence meant he was safe for the moment.

He could see that the rich smell of the food stirred them, the scorching hot tomato sauce with onions, pork chops and beans. Whatever else Doreen may have been, she was a skilled cook, who could make anything delicious.

Liam sat down next to Jason, across the table from Caroline. She smiled at him.

"Did you find your dog?" she asked.

Liam shook his head. He'd found no trace of Barney. Nothing on the cliff path, no sign Barney had returned to the house.

"I'll look again later," Liam said.

Caroline nodded.

"I'm sure he's fine. Dogs are smart. They always find their way home."

Liam said nothing. He needed to speak to Caroline and Jason. Urgent as it was, he knew he'd have to wait until later. He couldn't say anything with Steve and Doreen watching.

"Thank you for this meal," Caroline said, looking at her plate. "This smells wonderful."

"There's nothing like home cooking," Doreen said, handing Jason his plate. Who wants a drink?"

Jason said, "I'll take another beer."

"Caroline?"

"Just water for me, please."

Steve got the drinks. Then he and Doreen sat down at the table and everyone began to eat.

"This is wonderful," Caroline said after the first bite. "Scrumptious."

"Thank you."

"Nice painting," Caroline said, noticing a watercolour on the wall behind Liam. He didn't need to turn around to know which one she was talking about. The picture of the bungalow had hung on the wall for years.

Jason turned and looked at it.

"Huh," he said. "It's the same as the one on *that* wall."

Now it was Caroline's turn to look behind her, to where Jason was pointing. Another picture. Same composition, same colours, same bungalow. She said, "Are they identical?"

Doreen waved a warning finger at Caroline. "Be careful. You'll start Steve off on his favourite topic."

"What's that?"

"I painted one of them," Steve said. "The other is a copy. Can you tell which is which?"

Jason put down his fork and walked over to the picture behind him. "This is a real painting," he said. He walked over to other one, examining that too. "But so is this. They're both originals."

"Interesting way of looking at it," Steve said. He put a forkful of casserole in his mouth and waited until Jason sat down again before he continued. "I painted one in a burst of inspiration. A few weeks later, I copied it as precisely as I could."

Jason nodded. "So they're both originals, as I said."

"I wouldn't put it like that," Steve replied. "With the first one, I was excited. I was inspired. When I did the second one, I felt nothing. I was just copying."

"But you painted them both," Jason insisted. "You got a brush and applied paint onto a canvas?"

Steve leaned forward in his seat. "Let me ask you a question. Do you believe things have an essence?"

"What do you mean?"

"It's, you know, hard to define… something that sets one thing apart from another."

Jason frowned. "I don't follow."

"Like the difference between an original Van Gogh and a photocopy. They're completely different, right?"

Jason's lips curled into a sneer. "Sure. The original is worth twenty million euro. A copy might be worth ten."

He took a long drink of beer.

"Right." Steve said. "Why is that?"

Jason shrugged. "One is the real deal."

"But what *makes* it the real deal? It's the same picture. Looks the same on the wall, right? Shows the same thing. Uses the same colours. Why is one worth so much and one worth so little? Most people wouldn't be able to tell them apart if their lives depended on it."

"I'm not sure," Jason said slowly. "One was painted by a genius. The other was printed by a machine."

"So what?"

"So," Jason said, "one is real."

"What does that *mean*?"

Doreen took Steve's arm. "I'm sure these nice young people couldn't care less about your views on art."

Caroline smiled. "The question is interesting. It's about what you think the thing is, rather than what the thing actually is."

"Bullshit," Jason said, draining his beer bottle.

"I agree with Caroline," Doreen said. "Take a different example. This dinner, say. Do you like the pork?"

Jason nodded. His plate was almost empty, so clearly he was enjoying it.

"Absolutely delicious," Caroline said.

"Now what if I told you it isn't pork? What if I told you it was Barney, Liam's dog?"

Liam froze.

"What?" Jason said.

"What if I killed his dog and used its meat in the casserole? Would you feel differently about what you're eating?"

Jason said, "That would be disgusting."

"Why?" Doreen said. "You've been enjoying it up to now. Who cares if it's pig meat or dog meat? Maybe they taste the same. The only thing that's changed is your *idea* of what you're eating. Just like Caroline said."

Caroline laughed. "What an example."

"Sorry," Doreen said. "Bad illustration. I don't want to put you off your food. I used pork, by the way. Swear to god."

She laughed, then forked some casserole into her mouth. The others continued eating too, after taking a moment to put the image out of their minds.

But Liam couldn't.

His stomach was doing cartwheels. He fought the urge to vomit, but it was hard because he was sure what Doreen had said really was true. Barney was dead, and they were eating him. It was part of Liam's punishment.

Doreen gave him a nudge in the ribs.

"Eat up," she said.

CHAPTER SEVENTEEN

Caroline swallowed her last bite of casserole. Dinner had been delicious, though Doreen's joke about dog meat had been in bad taste, and almost put Caroline off it. She drained her glass of water and glanced at Jason, who was finishing his third beer.

I hope he doesn't drink any more, she thought.

Jason couldn't handle it. After a couple of drinks, he got surly, then sleepy, and finally, maudlin.

Steve cleared the empty plates away. Caroline tried to help him, but he shooed her away.

"Sit down, sit down," he said with a smile.

"Thank you, Steve. How's your head?"

"Much better."

Doreen stood up. "Who wants dessert?"

"I'd love some," Caroline said. She still had a little room left. Always did when it came to sweet things. Sugar was her weakness. "What is it?"

"Apple tart with ice cream."

Caroline swallowed, remembering the way Jason had stabbed his finger into the tart earlier.

"Lovely," Caroline said. She forced a smile.

"I'll take some too," Jason said.

"You want a beer with that?" Steve said. "Or maybe something stronger?"

"Sure."

"Both?" Steve laughed and headed over to the fridge. "Let's have a beer first. We can move onto the heavy stuff later. Nothing else to do."

Doreen brought the tart over and set it down in the middle of the table. The gaping hole in the pastry screamed at Caroline. It couldn't have been more obvious. Doreen and Steve would be furious with them for ruining dessert. She was surprised that Doreen hadn't said anything yet. Caroline braced herself for the coming rebuke.

Doreen got a long, sharp-looking knife.

Caroline glanced at Jason.

Will he apologise? No, he never does.

She didn't know whether to say something. She decided to wait and see what happened.

Doreen began to slice the tart, cutting it into six equal slices.

"Are you saving a slice for your other son?" Caroline asked.

"Of course," Doreen said. She glanced at Liam. "We can't forget about Frank."

"Where is he?"

"Visiting friends."

"I guess he won't be home tonight. I mean, with the weather being what it is."

Doreen nodded but said nothing. The knife sliced through the tart, right next to Jason's finger hole.

She must see it, Caroline thought. *She sees it, but she's too kind to mention it.*

Doreen put an intact piece of tart on Caroline's plate.

Caroline wanted to say thanks, but her throat was dry. Now the knife was slicing through the tart on the other side of the finger hole. Another intact slice went onto a plate for Jason. Doreen cut three more slices and plated them.

Finally, only one slice was left. The one for Frank. The one that Jason ruined.

It sat in the middle of the table, untouched, while they ate in dead silence.

CHAPTER EIGHTEEN

After dinner, Steve made tea for Caroline. It was not a brand Caroline liked but she wasn't going to complain. At least it warmed her.

Steve and Doreen drank bitter-smelling coffee. When Steve had finished his, he stood up and slapped Jason on the shoulder.

"Come to the sitting room," he said. "I have a nice bottle of whiskey I've been waiting to crack open. Might as well do it today."

"Now you're talking," Jason said.

He gave Caroline a shrug before disappearing down the hall.

Doreen began tidying up the dishes, piling them up by the sink. Liam sat sullenly at the kitchen table.

Caroline hated feeling useless, especially now that she was a guest in someone else's home. She didn't think she could look at the ruined slice of apple tart for another minute. She got to her feet.

"I'll wash the dishes," she said. "It's the least I can do."

"No need," Doreen replied. "It's Liam's turn. He'll do it."

"I can help, then."

"No. Liam will handle it. Won't you?"

The boy nodded. "Sure," he said.

Caroline wondered if he was feeling alright. His voice sounded thin, and his face was paler than it had been earlier.

"Caroline, you just take it easy," Doreen said. "I have some wine, if you'd like a glass?"

"No, thanks. I don't usually drink alcohol."

Doreen stared at her as if she'd never heard of such a thing before. "Oh?"

"I like to keep a clear head."

"Sensible." Doreen nodded slowly.

"You know what? I think I'll go to bed if that's alright with you," Caroline said.

"So early?"

"I'm a little tired. I'll try to catch some sleep. About our clothes—"

"They're already in the washing machine. Don't worry about a thing. In the morning, everything will be clean and dry, and Steve can help you with your car."

"Wonderful. I don't know how to thank you."

"Don't worry about it," Doreen said.

Caroline gave a little wave. "Well, good night."

"Night."

Caroline went to the bedroom. Her overnight bag was gone. Had it been in the room after her shower? Caroline couldn't remember. She was only sure that it had been wet. Maybe Doreen had put it in the washing machine too.

Caroline found her toilet bag on the dresser. She took it with her and went to the bathroom. The lacy underwear sat where she'd left them. Caroline shuddered. She had forgotten about them.

Everything over the last few hours seemed like a kind of dream. The first part had been exciting – driving through the natural beauty of the Cork landscape with her boyfriend, looking forward to the fun ahead. Valentine's Day in a nice hotel. The second part was more like a nightmare – the breakdown and the maniac driver in the SUV. At least, they had found the McGlynn house, though.

They were lucky.

Caroline brushed her teeth and went back to the bedroom. She turned on the bedside lamp.

A sheet of white paper, folded once, sat on top of her pillow. Caroline opened it and read the message scrawled in pen.

I need help. PLEASE DON'T TELL Steve and Doreen. Meet me outside at midnight.

CHAPTER NINETEEN

Once he'd left the note on Caroline's pillow, Liam hurried down the hall to the kitchen, wiping his sweaty hands on his T-shirt as he went.

He was gambling everything on a stranger's help. He had no choice. But if Caroline said anything to Steve or Doreen about the note… well, Liam didn't want to think about that.

He opened the door to the kitchen to find Doreen staring at him.

"Where were you?" she said.

"The toilet."

"Finish the dishes."

She sat at her usual chair at the kitchen table.

Liam wanted to ask about Barney, wanted Doreen to confirm his worst fear, that she had killed the dog to punish him, put its meat in a casserole and made him eat it. He desperately wanted to know for sure that his dog was not lost in the storm.

But he wasn't going to ask. Experience had taught him that Doreen would never tell him the truth. Instead, she'd draw out the agony and uncertainty for as long as possible, teasing and tormenting him.

He made his way to the sink and began washing the dishes.

"Make those plates clean enough to eat off," Doreen said. Her favourite joke.

Liam supposed he was seven when he started to wonder if his mother was evil. With his father, it happened a little later.

He remembered the magic trick Steve performed for Frank and him on their seventh birthday. Steve called it 'the duplicator'. He'd rigged up a bunch of old engine parts to look like a piece of fancy scientific equipment, and placed it in the sitting room. He also set up a curtain rail, with two red curtains. The curtains hid an area on each side of the machine.

Frank and Liam sat on the couch, eagerly waiting for the magic show to begin.

"Are you ready, boys?" Steve asked.

"Yeah," they shouted.

"I bought you a present, son." Steve was talking to Frank. He held up a goldfish bowl.

"Can I feed it?" Frank asked.

"Later. Right now I'm going to use this little guy to perform some magic."

Being the younger twin by a whole nine minutes, Liam never got the good presents, the good food, the hugs and kisses.

Steve made a big show of putting the goldfish bowl behind one of the red curtains, jiggling with his scientific 'apparatus', and announcing that the duplication had been successful. He pulled back the curtain on his right side, showing them Frank's goldfish again. He then revealed, with a flourish, what was behind the red curtain on the other side of the machine.

"Ta da," Steve said. He pulled back the curtain to show another goldfish in another bowl.

"There we are. An identical copy."

The boys looked at it in amazement, fully believing that he had really made a copy of the fish appear out of nowhere.

"Is it the same fish?" a grinning Steve asked the twins. He handed Frank the first fish bowl, then held up the second one for them both to examine.

"No," Frank said, squinting at the fish suspiciously.

"What do you think, Liam?"

"I'm not sure."

Frank punched him on the arm. "Who cares what he thinks? He's a copy too. He's just a copy of me."

Grinning, Steve handed Liam the second fish. "For you. A copy for a copy."

Liam might still have been haunted by that day, even if that was the only trick. But Steve hadn't finished with them yet.

"Let's duplicate something else," he said.

The twins went silent as they waited to hear what he would choose to copy next. That was when Doreen walked into the room. Immediately, Liam felt uncomfortable, like something terrible was going to happen.

"No," he said. "Don't."

Doreen back-handed him across the mouth. He fell back in the couch, too stunned to cry. When he sat up, his mother was stepping behind the curtain and his father was starting 'the duplicator' again. It began making noise, while Steve made a show of fiddling with the dials and switches.

Then the machine fell silent.

Steve watched the two boys' faces as he whipped away the red curtain to show their mother still standing where she had been before. Then he reached over the other side of the machine and pulled away the curtain there – to reveal another woman. She had Doreen's fleshy face and deep-set eyes, and she was dressed in the same cardigan and cotton pants.

"Hello boys," she said.

Even her voice was the same.

An identical copy of their mother.

Thinking of it now, as Liam washed the dishes in the kitchen, tears welled up in his eyes. It must have been awfully easy to fool a couple of kids, who had never been told that their mother had a twin sister.

Liam didn't learn the truth until that evening, when he overheard the sisters laughing about it over wine.

Yeah.

That was when he decided Doreen wasn't just mean.

She was evil.

CHAPTER TWENTY

Caroline sat on the bed and read the note again.

I need help. PLEASE DON'T TELL Steve and Doreen. Meet me outside at midnight.

Clearly the message had been written by Liam, but Caroline didn't know what to make of it. Was it a joke? Based on what Caroline had seen of the teenager, he didn't seem like the joking kind. If anything, he came across as depressed and anxious, like so many teenagers.

Like Caroline used to be.

There had been times as a teenager when she desperately felt the need to reach out to someone, even a stranger. Someone she thought would understand her. Was that what Liam was doing? Maybe he wanted to tell her something that he thought his parents wouldn't understand.

But why outside? Why at midnight?

The wind gusted against the window, moving the curtains slightly. She felt the breeze on her face. Single-glazed windows, out here? Amazing.

She put the sheet of paper on the nightstand and took off her jumper. Then she got under the duvet, still wearing Doreen's jeans and a T-shirt. Caroline was reluctant to take off the jeans, even in bed, since she wore nothing underneath. Not very comfortable, but she figured she could tolerate it for one night.

Her phone said it was nine thirty, still early. She left the lamp on and lay there, thinking this wasn't how her Valentine's Day was meant to turn out.

Caroline heard a door open in the hallway.

Her breathing quickened. She told herself not to be so silly. There was no reason to be scared. All the same, she reached out and turned off the bedside light. As footsteps approached her door, she pulled the duvet up to her chin.

The footsteps stopped outside her door.

Caroline held her breath. The handle began to move. Someone was coming in. Was it Liam? Perhaps he had decided he couldn't wait until midnight, and needed to speak to her now.

The door began to open.

Light from the hallway hit the wall beside the bed.

The door didn't creak, but Caroline heard the faint sound of its movement as it opened wider. The silhouette of a man appeared on the wall.

The man standing in the doorway.

Liam? Steve?

She swallowed. Waited.

"Caroline?"

She sat up at the sound of the whisper. "Jason?"

Flicking on the bedside light, she saw her boyfriend standing in the doorway. He smiled. "You okay?"

"Come in," she said. "Close the door."

He did. "What's up?"

"Nothing."

Jason looked half-drunk. She decided not to tell him about the note. If Liam's message was sincere, then they couldn't tell Doreen and Steve about it. But Jason, when he was drunk, was unable to keep a secret. Caroline couldn't trust him to keep the note to himself.

He came over to the bed and sat next to Caroline. She could smell the alcohol on his breath.

"Aren't you coming to bed?" she said.

"It's not even ten yet."

"I know, but what is there to do out here?"

"Exactly," Jason said. "There's nothing to do. The TV isn't working. The internet isn't working. We're just talking. Steve's telling funny stories."

"And you're getting drunk."

"We had a couple of glasses of whiskey."

"Is that a good idea? Why don't you come to bed?"

"Soon," Jason said. "Don't nag."

"Fine."

She turned away from him. Felt a flash of irritation when he put a hand on her hip.

Caroline said, "Don't even think about it."

"What did I do?"

"I'm not in the mood."

"Fine. Whatever," Jason said. "I thought it was Valentine's Day."

He stood up and left the room, closing the door behind him.

Caroline set the alarm on her phone for 23:50, then closed her eyes. She figured Jason was one drink away from getting belligerent. She hoped he wouldn't get them kicked out of the house.

CHAPTER TWENTY-ONE

Liam wanted to go into the sitting room, where Steve and Jason were talking. There might be an opportunity to talk to Jason alone if Steve had to use the toilet. But when he got up, Doreen told him sharply to stay where he was.

Perhaps she knew what he was thinking.

He hoped Caroline heeded his note.

What a Valentine's Day.

Liam would have loved to talk to Emily, but his phone had no signal. Should he have continued on to Emily's house earlier?

Overthinking plagued him, but he couldn't stop doing it.

Should he feel guilty for involving Caroline and Jason? He didn't want to put them in danger, but he had to save his own skin. He needed a way out.

Doreen looked up from her newspaper.

She said, "That girl doesn't love you. Don't kid yourself."

Liam bristled. He hated to hear Doreen talk about Emily. It was as if she sullied his girlfriend just by mentioning her.

"You don't know Emily."

"I know you," Doreen said. "Honestly, no one likes a loser."

She turned back to her newspaper.

Liam wanted to shout at her, but he didn't.

Be patient. Tonight everything will end.

Liam had no idea what his life would look like the next day, but he was sure it would be completely different. And it couldn't be any worse. He only needed to survive the coming hours.

It sounded like Steve was doing a good job of getting Jason roaring drunk. Their voices echoed down the hall from the sitting room. Jason was slurring his words, but Steve had a constitution that Hunter S. Thompson would have envied.

All Liam's hopes rested in Caroline alone.

CHAPTER TWENTY-TWO

Caroline had no idea when she fell asleep but, at some stage, she must have, because she woke when Jason staggered into the room. He pushed the door open too hard, smashing it into the wall behind.

"Caroline? I love you," Jason slurred.

Caroline's head was foggy with sleep. Jason turned on the ceiling light and staggered over to the bed. Caroline shielded her eyes.

"Would you turn that off?"

"I'm sorry, but I love you. I love you, Caroline. I'm saying it."

"Be quiet. Would you close the door?"

Jason laughed. "I love the way you close doors, Caroline. I love—"

"Shush. You can love me tomorrow."

Jason pushed the door shut. "Caroline, I love the way you shush me. No one could shush me the way you do."

"You're so drunk."

"Are you wearing the panties, Caroline?"

"What? That was you?" Caroline sat up in the bed. "I nearly blamed Liam."

Jason burst out laughing. "It's Valentine's Day."

"Oh my god. Are you coming to bed?"

Jason shrugged. "I don't know. I'd like to stay up, but we drank all the whiskey. I drank most of it, actually."

"I can smell it from here." Caroline turned on the bedside lamp. "Come and lie down."

Jason turned off the ceiling light and staggered over. He threw himself on the mattress next to her. The frame groaned beneath him.

"For god's sake, don't break the bed," Caroline told him.

"Don't worry. They're fine people. Steve is a fine guy. He didn't mind me drinking his whiskey to the last drop. A real gent."

Now that she was awake, Caroline realised she needed to use the bathroom. She swung her legs over the side of the bed. The floor was cool under her bare feet.

Jason blinked in surprise. "Where are you going?"

"I'll be back in a second."

"See if you can find some whiskey."

"You've had more than enough. You'll feel rotten in the morning."

Caroline walked out of the room to the sound of Jason's drunken laughter. The house was quiet. She had no idea of the time. Before midnight anyway, as her alarm had not yet sounded.

She crept to the bathroom, moving as silently as she could, though she was sure that Steve and Doreen were not yet in bed. Surely, they wouldn't turn in for the night before Jason.

The lacy underwear sat where she'd left them. Caroline stuffed them in the bin, then used the toilet, washed her hands and stepped into the hallway again.

The house was still.

Caroline walked up the hall. She stopped outside Frank's room, the room she was meant to steer clear of.

He's very private. Very particular about his personal space.

That was what Doreen had said.

A thought struck Caroline. What if Frank was in the house? What if he was in his room right now? Caroline's skin prickled. Could she feel the presence of another person nearby? Or was her imagination playing tricks on her?

There was no light under the door.

But a red stain was visible on the floor.

Caroline crouched down. Some red liquid seemed to have dried on the floor just under the door. Her first thought was—

"Can I help you?"

"Shit." Caroline jumped.

Doreen stood in the doorway to the kitchen. "What are you doing?"

Her tone was like that of Caroline's old geography teacher, who liked to ask the class questions she already knew the answers to.

"I... I thought I heard something in that room."

"Impossible. Frank isn't here."

Doreen began to walk down the hall as Caroline got to her feet.

Caroline glanced at the floor. "Yes. Of course. It must have been the wind."

Suddenly, it seemed important to get back to her bedroom. Doreen took a step down the hall. Caroline took a step up it. Her heart was racing. The spare bedroom lay halfway between them.

Doreen said, "I told you to leave Frank's room alone."

Caroline was nearly at the door.

So was Doreen.

"Yes, sorry. It was the wind. The sound I heard. Good night."

Caroline grabbed the handle and scrambled into the bedroom. Slamming the door, she pressed her back against it until she heard Doreen walking away.

CHAPTER TWENTY-THREE

Doreen stepped into the kitchen and closed the door behind her. She paused there and shook her head.

"What is it?" Liam said, his voice low. He wasn't sure he wanted to know the answer.

Doreen walked to the door leading to the other hall.

"Come with me," she said.

Liam got to his feet. Slowly he followed his mother down the corridor. Doreen ducked her head into the sitting room and spoke to Steve in a low voice. Then she made for the laundry room.

Liam followed.

What was this about?

As soon as he stepped inside the laundry room, Doreen backhanded him across the face.

"What did you say to that girl?"

She hit him again, but not before he got his hands up. He managed to block the blow.

"What did you tell her?"

"Nothing!"

"Don't lie to me."

"I'm not."

"I bet you told her lies about us."

Liam turned to run but Steve was right behind him. He smashed his fist into Liam's throat.

Gasping for breath, Liam dropped to his knees.

"Tie him up," Doreen said, handing Steve a length of thick hemp rope. She prised Liam's jaws apart and stuffed another piece of rope between his teeth, while Steve bound his hands behind his back.

"Where should we put him?"

Doreen pointed to the wall next to the washing machine. The farthest place from the door. Steve dragged Liam there and shoved him down, so Liam was sitting on the concrete floor with his back against the wall. Both the wall and the floor were freezing cold.

Doreen came and stood in front of him.

"You just killed that girl. You might as well have slit her throat yourself. Her boyfriend too."

Liam's eyes went wide. He tried to shout, but he could only grunt.

"Are you happy with yourself? You killed them both. I told you to keep your loser mouth shut, and you couldn't even do that. You want to get us in trouble?"

Liam tried to speak again, but it was useless. Tears streamed down his face.

"What do you think we should do with him?" Steve asked.

"We'll have plenty of time to think of that once our guests have been dealt with."

"Right you are."

Steve kissed Doreen on the lips. They killed the light when they went out, leaving Liam in the dark.

CHAPTER TWENTY-FOUR

Caroline lay in bed in the darkness. Next to her, Jason, still fully clothed, snored loudly. Caroline's stomach churned, unnerved after her encounter with Doreen.

An hour later, she still couldn't settle. It was hard to pinpoint why she was so anxious. Doreen hadn't threatened her. But she picked up a weird vibe.

Caroline thought of Frank's room. Was the stain on the floor blood? That was what Caroline had been wondering when Doreen surprised her. And, if it was, what did that mean?

A rumbling sound came from outside.

Caroline strained to hear, but that was difficult with Jason's snoring. She gave him a punch on the arm.

He groaned. Slowly, his eyes opened.

"What was that for?"

"Listen," Caroline said. She flicked on the bedside lamp.

Jason rubbed his eyes. "I don't hear anything."

"It sounded like... like an engine."

"Huh?"

"Maybe a car or van."

Jason sighed and sat up. His eyelids were heavy. "We're a long way from the road."

"Not on the road. It was right outside."

"I doubt it."

Caroline said, "Seriously. I think they're doing something out there."

"Like what?"

Caroline had no idea. She checked the time on her phone. 23:45. Her midnight rendezvous was meant to happen in fifteen minutes.

She turned off her alarm. There was no need for it now.

Was the sound made by Liam? What could he possibly be doing?

"I'm going to take a look outside," Caroline said.

"What?"

"You stay here."

Jason wiped the sleep out of his eyes. He swung his legs over the side of the bed. "No, I'll go."

"I'm not helpless. I'm perfectly capable—"

"It's not that. I want to have a smoke," Jason said.

"Be careful."

Jason chuckled, stretching his arms out, and rubbing his eyes again. "I'm not going far."

"I don't like this."

Jason leaned over and kissed Caroline's cheek.

"I'll have a quick cigarette and see what's happening. Alright?"

Caroline nodded. She watched Jason stagger out of the bedroom.

Outside, the engine noise had stopped.

Everything was silent.

CHAPTER TWENTY-FIVE

Jason flicked on the kitchen light and looked around for his jacket, but he couldn't see it anywhere. Before he went to bed, Doreen had said that his clothes had been washed, and were in the dryer, so they'd be ready to wear first thing in the morning. Maybe she'd put his muddy jacket in the wash too.

The cold air might be nice, Jason decided. He knew he was very drunk, and the sensation was no longer pleasant.

He opened the door and stepped outside. Slushy snow splashed under his feet. Shivering, he fished a cigarette out of the packet in his jeans and lit it. Caroline must have imagined the engine. Jason couldn't hear anything like that. Nevertheless, he walked around the side of the house.

A blazing light caught his attention as he rounded the corner. The garage doors were wide open, revealing the huge interior. The first thing he saw was a gleaming black SUV. It looked like the one he and Caroline had encountered on the road.

The one that nearly killed them.

Caroline's Peugeot stood next to it. Its back wheels rested on the ground. The front wheels were hoisted up, attached to a white tow truck.

The cigarette fell out of Jason's mouth.

Steve had said he wouldn't be able to tow their car off the road tonight. Doreen had said that too. But here it was.

Jason wondered what else Doreen and Steve might have lied about. He thought of Steve's injury, and Liam's face – pale and scared the whole evening.

"Take him now."

Jason spun towards the voice, as a wrench smashed into the side of his skull with a sickening crunch of bone. He dropped to his hands and knees.

Steve and Doreen stood over him.

"Again," Doreen said.

Jason looked up. "No. Wait—"

Another blow, and everything went black.

CHAPTER TWENTY-SIX

The laundry room had a small window above the washing machine. It let a little light in, but the room was still dark. In that darkness, Liam struggled to free his hands.

The rough rope binding his wrists together dug into his skin. But he struggled on, trying to work his way free. He thought he was beginning to make progress when the door opened.

He froze as the light came on.

Steve stepped into the room, dragging Jason by the legs.

He was unconscious.

Or worse.

Liam groaned. He tried to speak but the rope in his mouth stopped him.

Breathing hard with the exertion, Steve pulled Jason across the floor. Jason's face scraped against the concrete.

Doreen stepped into the room and put her hands on her hips.

"This is all your fault," she said.

Steve let go of Jason, dropping him in the corner of the room, face-down.

"Shit. He was heavy for such a skinny guy," Steve said. Panting, he straightened up. "I really feel like a whiskey. Wish I hadn't let that bastard drink it all."

Doreen said, "Let's have a smoke. Then we can take care of the other one."

Steve nodded and followed Doreen out the door.

Before the door closed, Doreen stuck her head back in.

"I hope you're happy with yourself," she sneered. "You killed three people today. You just sit here and think about that."

The door shut and the light flicked off.

CHAPTER TWENTY-SEVEN

The longer Caroline waited for Jason to come back to bed, the more fearful she became. She sat up, nightmarish scenarios running through her mind. A few minutes ago, she'd thought she heard voices. Perhaps it was the wind, though. Or Jason, who was drunk. He might have been talking to himself while he smoked yet another cigarette.

Caroline's phone said it was midnight. Time for her to meet Liam. Had Jason run into him already?

She stepped out of the bed, found her shoes and opened the door to the corridor. Lights out, doors closed. No sign of anyone. She continued to the kitchen. The light was on, but there was no sign of anyone.

Caroline found the back door unlocked.

She stepped outside.

Feeling sick with fright, she walked alongside the building, passing the window to the spare bedroom, then the window to Frank's room.

She stopped and stepped on the tips of her toes, so she could look inside the window. On the other side of the glass, the curtains were closed, but there was a gap of about an inch where they didn't meet.

Caroline could make out a shape on the floor, but she wasn't sure what it was. The room was so dark. She waited for her vision to adjust to the darkness. Slowly the shape came into focus.

A body lay at the foot of the bed. It was covered by a blanket, but the shape was distinct.

Caroline felt a pulse of horror. Was that Frank?

Behind her, the kitchen door opened.

Caroline ran to the corner and flung herself around it. She was outside the bathroom now, and out of sight of Doreen and Steve, but she heard them talking. They seemed to be standing outside the kitchen door.

Caroline closed her eyes and tried to regain control of herself. Her chest rose and fell, her breathing panicked.

They must have killed him.

Their own son.

That explained why they didn't want her going into his room – and why they'd seemed so wary when she and Jason arrived. They were afraid of their secret getting out. If they'd do such a thing, they'd also kill Caroline and Jason to stop them talking.

Where *was* Jason?

She took a deep breath and ran in the opposite direction to Doreen and Steve. Coming to the garage, she caught sight of the black SUV that had nearly hit her.

Then she saw her Peugeot.

Caroline sprinted to the garage. She might be able to get away by car. The Peugeot was useless, of course. Steve must have brought it here on the tow truck, but presumably the car had not been repaired yet. She noticed a machine standing next to the Peugeot. A wet vacuum cleaner. What the hell did Steve plan to do with that?

Never mind, Caroline told herself.

The Range Rover was her ticket out of here. She ran over to it and tried its doors, but they were locked. The key fob must be in the house, or in Steve's pocket.

The tow truck was locked too.

"Okay," Caroline whispered.

New plan.

She needed to find the keys to one of the cars, and she needed to find Jason. Once she did that, the two of them could get away from this place.

She remembered passing a laundry room when they entered the house earlier. There had been a key rack on the wall.

She ran along the side of the house until she found the right window. She got on the tips of her toes and peered inside.

Liam was tied up on the floor.

Beside him, Jason lay still on the floor.

The sight of this new horror did not make Caroline back away. It made her more determined to get inside. She had to find out if Jason was alright.

She dragged a flower box over to the window and stepped up onto it. With her elbow, she smashed the window, hoping the sound would not carry on the wind. The blow hurt, but she ignored the pain.

She pulled herself up onto the narrow windowsill and jumped down into the room.

CHAPTER TWENTY-EIGHT

The breaking glass startled Liam. He craned his neck to the side so he could see the window. Caroline climbed through. She dropped to the floor, crossed the room and fumbled around for the light switch. The room lit up.

She went to Jason, dropping on her knees next to him.

"Jason?"

She shook his body. No response. Nothing. Liam saw the look on Caroline's face. Her boyfriend was dead – and it was Liam's fault.

She took a moment, then came over to Liam and hunkered down in front of him. The rough rope was wedged tight in his mouth. She worked it out slowly. When she was done, Liam gasped for breath.

"Tell me what's going on," Caroline said.

Liam looked at the door to the hall.

"They might have heard the glass break."

"Then you better speak quickly."

"Okay."

She untied his hands while he filled her in.

It had started before lunch, when Frank found the Valentine's Day card that Liam had made for Emily.

Somehow Liam had kept his relationship with her a secret for three months. He didn't want his family to know. But Frank had sensed that *something* was up. He searched Liam's room and found the card with a poem Liam had written for her.

Of course, Frank read it aloud to Steve and Doreen while they ate lunch. And the three of them laughed at it.

Frank refused to give the card back. He took it to his room, and Liam followed.

"Emily Brown?" Frank said, smiling at the thought. "You and Emily Brown?"

The three of them went to the same school, and it irritated Liam that Frank knew who she was. Normally Liam stifled his habitual feelings. Rage. Fear. Self-loathing. Why not? Doreen and Steve always made sure that Liam knew he was a loser.

He'd become accustomed to their cruelty, had accepted it as normal – at least, until Emily told him, *Some people shouldn't be allowed to be parents.*

Doreen hated the fact that she herself was a twin. She was delighted when Frank came along. He was the perfect little son she'd always wanted. Not so happy when Liam followed nine minutes later. An unwanted freebie. Identical, but not the same.

When Liam followed Frank to his room, adrenaline was pulsing through his body. He wasn't sure he could control his feelings.

"Are you going to give her your card now?" Frank asked.

"None of your business."

"What if I meet her instead?" Frank grinned. "I bet she'll never know the difference."

Liam's anger began spin out of control. He welcomed the feeling. He wanted to hurt Frank, wanted Frank to be the one who suffered, for once. Frank held the card high in the air and teased Liam like he was a kid.

Liam lost it then.

His first punch hit Frank in the side, below the ribs. It made Frank double over, dropping the card on the floor.

"You're dead," Frank said. His voice was icy, and Liam realised it was no figure of speech.

Liam tried to leave the room, but Frank grabbed him from behind. They struggled and fell into the mirrored door of Frank's wardrobe. The mirror shattered, falling to the floor around them in jagged shards.

Liam scrambled to his feet, but Frank was faster. He pulled the lace out of his shoe, wrapped it around Liam's neck and began to strangle him with it.

"I'm going to go and meet Emily. I'm going to have a real good time with her," Frank whispered in his ear.

Liam smashed the back of his head into Frank's nose. The impact made a horrible crunch. Frank dropped the lace.

"You're so fucking dead," Frank shouted.

Liam tried to crawl away across the carpeted floor, but Frank grabbed his leg and flipped him onto his back. Frank sat on Liam's chest, driving the air out of him, and pulled a switchblade out of his jeans.

"Get off me," Liam said.

"Shut up."

Many times, Frank had threatened him with this blade. Many more times, he had stabbed him with it, or cut him with it. Small wounds, Liam supposed, but they all added up.

The sight of a knife now made Liam frantic. Frank's eyes were wild as he pressed the button on the knife and the blade shot out.

"No," Liam said.

"Shut up."

Liam reached out for something, anything, on the floor. His fingers touched a long shard from the mirror. His only hope.

Frank was drawing back his arm, preparing to stab the knife into Liam's neck.

Liam had no choice.

He grabbed the piece of broken mirror and thrust it as hard as he could into Frank's side. It went in deep

Frank looked down at the wound in surprise. Liam pulled out the shard and stabbed it into Frank again. The knife fell from Frank's hand. He gasped, then keeled over.

That was when Doreen and Steve tore into the room.

"What have you done?" Doreen screamed.

Liam backed away. He'd killed the one they loved. There was no telling what would happen now.

Steve hurried over to Frank, who was taking his last breath. He cradled him in his arms. Doreen got on her knees and touched Frank's face, but the life was already draining out of it.

Liam ran out the door.

He took Steve's Range Rover and drove off with the vague idea of going to Emily's house and asking her to elope. Along the way, he realised what a stupid idea it was. But if he didn't do that, what could he do? Where could he go?

Nowhere.

Eventually, he turned around and started driving home. That was when he came across Caroline and Jason at the petrol station. All he knew was he needed help. If he went home alone, he thought Doreen and Steve would kill him.

So he sabotaged the Peugeot. Nothing to feel guilty about. He figured a wet vac would get the gravel out later and make the engine run again.

Caroline and Jason were heading in the direction of the McGlynn house anyway. It was the only house around, so if their car broke down nearby, they'd probably come to the McGlynns looking for help.

He panicked when he met them on the road. Of course, he should have picked them up and brought them to the house himself, but he drove straight past.

When Liam got home, Steve had come after him. Liam smashed Steve in the face with a torch. Then he'd gone down the cliff road looking for Barney. When he came back to the house, Caroline and Jason had arrived.

And by then everything was hurtling towards disaster.

CHAPTER TWENTY-NINE

Liam spoke quickly, avoiding eye contact as he did so. When he stopped, Caroline sensed that there was much more he wanted to say. He had only given her the briefest account of what happened, but that would have to be enough for now.

"I'm so sorry," Liam said, looking up for the first time. "I didn't want to cause you trouble. I just needed help. I didn't know what to do."

"You should have reported the accident."

Liam nodded. "I should have but I didn't. They think I told you what happened."

"What if you did tell me? Why are they so worried about that?"

Liam shrugged. "I guess they're afraid of what I might say – about how they treated me over the years. They aren't nice people," he added.

"I don't understand why they let us in at all," Caroline said.

"It would have looked suspicious if they turned you away. And maybe they wondered if you already knew something."

Caroline thought she should have felt colder towards Liam. But he hadn't killed Jason. Doreen and Steve had. And what happened with Frank? It was almost understandable. She squeezed his shoulder.

"Let's get out of here." She helped him to his feet and they walked over to the key rack. "Are the key fobs for the cars here?"

Liam shook his head. "Steve has them."

Caroline heard footsteps in the hall. Moving fast. "They're coming."

"Go out the window."

Liam boosted Caroline. She crawled through the window, out into the night. The lights of the garage still blazed. She turned and held out a hand to Liam as he crawled through the window after her.

Behind him, the door burst open.

Steve saw them and ran across the room. He grabbed at Liam's foot, but Liam kicked out hard, smashing his runner into Steve's face. Steve fell on his ass. Caroline pulled Liam as he scrambled out the window.

"You're going to pay," Doreen screamed. "You ungrateful little shit."

Liam dropped to the ground next to Caroline. If it was possible, his face had turned a shade paler.

He's only seventeen, Caroline reminded herself. *And that's his mother.*

A chill, which had nothing to do with the cold, passed through her.

"Come on," she said, and set off running for the garage, holding her loose jeans up with one hand. She wished she had a jacket, but there was nothing she could do about that.

"We can't take a car."

"I don't want those fuckers to be able to take one either."

She ran through the open doorway. Tools hung on hooks on one wall. Every kind imaginable. Too many.

"I need something sharp," Caroline said.

Liam pulled a chisel off the wall and handed it to her. He took another one himself, and ran to the SUV, where he burst two of the tyres.

Caroline burst two of the tow truck's tyres.

Voices nearby.

"Let's go," Caroline called. They threw down the tools and ran outside. Steve and Doreen were jogging towards them from the house. Caroline was in good shape. Liam looked like he was too. They would be able to outrun the older couple.

Caroline hurried across the driveway, towards the yew tree and the road that led away from the house. They needed to keep running.

And then?

Caroline didn't know.

Behind her, Liam called out. She turned to see that he had tripped. Doreen and Steve were closing in on him.

Steve held a wrench in his hand, and he looked like he meant to use it.

CHAPTER THIRTY

Caroline didn't want to lose any time, but she forced herself to run back where Liam had fallen. She took his hand and helped him to his feet as Steve reached them.

Teeth clenched, he swung the wrench at Liam's head, missing by an inch. Then they were running again, Caroline still holding her jeans up, so she didn't trip too.

"Are you okay?" Caroline said.
"Yeah. Just run," Liam shouted.
She headed towards the road.
"Not that way," he said. "To the cliff."
"Are you crazy?"
"Trust me."
"I don't want to die."
"Neither do I."

Liam ran in a wide curve around Steve and Doreen.

Reluctantly, Caroline followed.

They passed the house and turned down a mud trail that ran along the cliff face. The Atlantic Ocean roared. A terrifying drop, only six feet away, on their left side. Caroline followed in Liam's footsteps, jogging now rather than running, to reduce the risk of tripping. No point getting away from Doreen and Steve if she was going to let her own panic get her killed.

She could barely think. Knowing that there was such a huge drop right beside her? That short-circuited her brain. Dizzy as it made her, she kept going.

The cliff face was uneven, and the path roughly followed its contours, generally remaining about six feet from the precipice. On the other side, the ground sloped upwards.

"We're nearly there," Liam shouted over his shoulder.

"Nearly where?"

Liam pointed ahead. A picnic table stood in the grass at the side of the path, about twenty feet from the cliff edge.

"Steve put it there years ago. It's his favourite place to smoke."

Great, Caroline thought.

"The weather was good yesterday," Liam said.

"So what?" Caroline shouted, wondering if he was demented.

"So I was cycling. I left my bike there."

Sure enough, a mountain bike was chained to the table. Caroline doubted that the chain was there to prevent theft. Perhaps it was to secure the bike against the ferocious wind. As she drew closer, she saw that the picnic table too was secured. Each leg was encased in cement, which in turn was attached to a rocky outcrop. She figured that was why it hadn't flown into the sea during a storm.

Liam unlocked the bike and ran with it back to the path. Caroline followed.

"Get on," he said.

"Are you kidding me?"

"If we can make it to the end of this path, we'll come out on the road you were driving on earlier. This is a shortcut."

Caroline shook her head.

In the distance, she heard the roar of an engine.

"That can't be a car..." she said.

The path was too narrow. A car would never make it down here. And anyway, they had burst the tyres.

Liam shrugged. "Maybe they didn't notice the tyres. Or maybe they don't care. They're crazy. They'll do anything to get me." He swung his leg over the saddle and looked back at her. "Are you coming?"

She got on behind him and wrapped her arms around his waist. He kicked off and began pedalling furiously. At first the bike wobbled from side to side. Caroline unleashed a stream of curses and closed her eyes, but she found that was even scarier, so she opened them again.

The cliff was so close... but the ground to the right looked too rough to cycle on. An obstacle course of rock and grass. They had to stick to the path.

The sound of the engine grew louder and headlights swept over them. Caroline squeezed Liam tighter.

"They're coming! Pedal faster."

His legs worked frantically. Caroline struggled to hold on as the bike bumped along. She could hear waves crashing at the foot of the cliff. Ahead, the ground rose in a hill.

Caroline risked a glance behind her. The Range Rover was shooting towards them. The vehicle was a crazy angle, with its left wheels on the path, and its right wheels up on the sloping ground next to the path.

It was extremely close. Its deflated front tyres slapped against the ground.

Doreen was sitting in the passenger seat, her trout-like face dark. Behind the wheel, Steve's face was twisted with rage.

The Range Rover was closing the gap.

It was nearly upon them.

"Faster," Caroline screamed in Liam's ear.

He huffed and puffed as they rose the hill ahead. Despite his efforts, they were moving slower and slower. They'd never get away.

"Hold on," Liam shouted as they approached the crest of the hill.

"What?"

The Range Rover came so close that Caroline thought she could feel the heat from the engine.

It was moving so fast. Soon it would crush them.

"Hold on!" Liam shouted.

They reached the top of the hill. On the other side, the path turned right, following the contour of the cliff. Liam wrenched the handlebars to the side. Both Liam and Caroline tumbled to the ground, hitting it hard on their left side. The bike fell on top of them, stabbing Caroline in the ribs.

She gasped.

They rolled onto the grass.

Caroline only saw Doreen and Steve for a second as the Range Rover crested the hill. Steve was wrestling with the wheel, but it was too late. They were moving too fast and the ruined tyres made it impossible for them to correct their course in time.

The Range Rover launched into the air.

Its back wheels landed on the ground, but the front ones were spinning in space. Tipping forward.

The Range Rover tumbled over the side of the cliff and careened out of sight, into the darkness of the ocean.

CHAPTER THIRTY-ONE

It took forty minutes to cycle to the nearest town, if you could call it a town. Nothing more than a cluster of a few dozen houses, one pub, one shop, and a closed-down post office. All together along one road.

It was after 1:00 and everything was closed, but Liam rang the doorbell of a neat little house with a garden full of daffodils.

"We'll do this right," Caroline said. "Okay?"

"Okay," Liam said. He rang the bell a few more times. Emily and her parents would be asleep.

For a while after Doreen and Steve plunged to their deaths, Caroline and Liam sat on the freezing ground, looking out to sea. Liam cried. Caroline couldn't imagine what he felt. Her own feelings were enough of a jumble for her to try and sort out. Horror at the day's events, grief over Jason's death, disbelief at the cruelty of which people were capable, and, now, relief at their escape.

Liam wiped his eyes. He said, "They'll arrest me for what happened to Frank. I should disappear and never come back. I don't want to go to jail."

Caroline shook her head.

"You're young. What happened with Frank was an accident. Don't ruin your life by making the wrong choice now. Do you want to run forever? Do you think Emily would want that?"

There was a long silence while Liam thought.

"I don't know," he said finally.

"Trust that things will turn out alright."

"I don't trust anyone."

"Not even me?" Caroline said.

He shrugged. "Maybe a little."

"Then trust me when I say, I won't leave you alone. Whatever happens next."

"You don't need to babysit me. You're not my Mum."

"I know. Thank fuck for that, right?"

Liam cracked a smile. "Yeah."

"After what we've been through, I reckon you could say we're friends."

They shook hands in the dark.

"Yeah," Liam said again. "Okay."

"Good. Tell the truth. Unburden yourself once and for all. Then you can start thinking about a new life. You might need therapy," Caroline added with a smile.

Liam blew his nose. "I guess so. I'm pretty messed up."

"You're not the only one."

Neither of them had their phone and Liam said he didn't want to go back to the house, didn't want to spend another minute in that place.

So they'd continued down the track, pushing the bike, until they came out on the road. Then they mounted the bike and cycled to Emily's house.

After seven rings of the doorbell, her father opened the door in his dressing gown.

"What on earth is going on?"

"I'm sorry to wake you, but we need to use your phone," Caroline said.

The man turned on the porch light and looked at their faces.

"What's this about?"

Caroline said, "It's an emergency."

A teenage girl in fluffy pink pyjamas appeared behind the man. She had the kindest brown eyes Caroline had seen in a long time. She hurried past her father and threw her arms around Liam.

"Are you okay?" she said. "What happened?"

"It's a long story."

Caroline realised they must look awful. Covered in mud and blood. Clothes ruined. A trail of destruction behind them.

She and Liam *were* friends now. They had gone through hell together, and they had come out the other side.

Caroline smiled. "You must be Emily."

The girl nodded.

"How did you know?"

Caroline didn't reply. She hoped Liam remembered the poem he had written for this girl, because she looked like someone who'd appreciate it. And that was worth more than he probably knew.

THE END

THE HOSTAGE

CHAPTER ONE

Night is falling as Dean Cullen sprints up the lane. The pale sky is dimming. His footsteps echo off the garage doors on each side. He needs to hide. Darkness will help, but his orange jacket is a problem. It's like a beacon.

As the soles of his shoes slap against the ground, he hears shouting behind him. He glances back. At the end of the lane, a patrol car with flashing lights is stuck behind a parked van.

A helicopter approaches from the distance, and Dean knows it's after him too.

Hard to imagine how things could have gone worse.

He needs to disappear.

Another lane intersects the one he's on. He takes the corner fast and hopes there's a way out ahead. He isn't familiar with this part of Dublin. There are a lot of big houses, and the place seems to be strewn with embassies. Solid, stone walls line both sides of the lane, and Dean suspects that gardens lie on the other side.

As a twenty-five-year-old, who hit Mountjoy Prison's gym at least five times a week until recently, Dean is in good shape. But he's still gasping for breath. Maybe he's in shock.

One foot in front of the other.

Go, go, go.

He's already been running for five minutes, since crashing the Toyota, and his body is flooded with adrenaline.

He hears the creak of a door opening.

Ahead, a figure appears out of a doorway, pushing a bicycle. Lean, lanky, face hidden by a hoodie, dressed all in black – Dean decides it's a teenage boy. The boy starts to push the bike in the other direction.

Dean shouts, "Wait."

The boy turns around, his eyes widening as Dean approaches, looking at his fluorescent orange jacket, the blood-spattered T-shirt, the expression on Dean's face.

The boy takes a couple of steps away, still pushing the bike, as if he's thinking of fleeing. But Dean has already reached him.

"How much for your hoodie?"

"What?"

Dean doubles over, gasping for breath. His mouth has the metallic taste of blood and he's not sure it's his own. After everything that has happened, he feels strangely calm. He takes a few deep breaths, then straightens up.

The kid looks younger than he thought. Thirteen or fourteen. A spotty face, a peach-fuzz moustache and watery eyes.

"The hoodie," Dean says. "How much?"

"I don't—"

"What's your name?"

"Karl."

"Alright, Karl, I need your hoodie. And I don't have time to mess around." Dean pulls out his wallet. He has eighty euro inside, in four notes. He shoves the money into the boy's hands, then tears off his jacket. "You can have mine."

The sound of the helicopter's blades draws nearer. And that's not the only sound Dean hears. The dull drumming of boots, the metallic crunch of machine guns.

They're catching up.

Karl stands staring at him.

I had to get a freezer, Dean thinks. He's observed that there are only three kinds of people in the world. Dean pigeon-holes them depending on how they react when everything goes to hell. There are those who act. There are those who call for help. And there are those who freeze. Karl is a freezer.

"I have about five seconds to complete this transaction – and I'm not taking no for an answer."

The kid stares at the money.

"For my hoodie?"

"And I have a job for you. Put on my jacket and cycle away from here as fast as you can."

Karl shrugs off his hoodie and hands it to Dean.

"Where should I go?" he asks.

"I don't care. Just keep going."

"Until when?"

"Until they stop you."

Karl looks at the orange jacket. "This isn't my style."

Dean slips on the black hoodie. He says, "I don't care."

The boy's eyes linger on the bloodstains on Dean's T-shirt.

"Go," Dean says.

The boy puts on the jacket and gets on the bike. Dean watches him cycle up the lane, picking up speed as he goes.

The helicopter looms into view overhead. Its searchlight blazes into action, illuminating a nearby area.

Dean has to get out of sight.

Running over to the nearest wall, he jumps up, grabs the top of the wall, and pulls himself up.

As he hoped, a garden lies on the other side. A three-floor, brown-brick house stands at the other end of the garden. Nothing in the garden but grass and a small shed.

No one around.

Dean drops to the ground, glad the grass provides a soft landing. He smells soil on the air. Sees daffodils and tulips at the side of the garden.

A lovely March evening.

As Dean jogs up the garden to the house, he runs his fingers over the semi-automatic pistol tucked into the waistband of his jeans.

CHAPTER TWO

Lindsey O'Reilly is washing the dishes after dinner when she hears a helicopter. Nothing unusual about that. Traffic helicopters pass overhead occasionally. Sometimes she also sees the red and white Coast Guard helicopter as it heads out towards Dublin Bay.

This is different.

A column of light blazes down from the dimming sky, illuminating the rooftops of houses behind her. A search helicopter.

What's going on?

She leans over the sink to get a better look, brushing her long hair over her shoulder, but the helicopter has moved directly overhead, and she can see nothing.

Oh god, Lindsey thinks. *Who are they chasing? What's happening?*

Born in Aberdeen, Washington, twenty years earlier, Lindsey has always been a worrier. Maybe because she's the youngest of four girls. It's like she was always worried about being forgotten. Lindsey's Mom jokes that her first words were, "I'm scared".

Well, maybe now there's a reason to be anxious.

Anxiety affects Lindsay's stomach. Her sisters are like that too. When Lindsey's grandmother died, they all had terrible bellyaches for days.

At dinnertime, Lindsey overate, finding her own pasta carbonara too delicious to leave on the plate. Now, the *whoomp whoomp* of the helicopter blades sends a wave of nausea through her. Lindsey has to fight it, or she'll end up being sick in the bathroom.

She peers out the window but still can't see anything.

Her apartment is at the back of the building, on the second floor, as Lindsey thinks of it, though Irish people call that the first floor. Whatever. Her place has a good view of the garden. Lindsey is lucky because some of the building's other apartments have no view at all.

Noticing that she's dripping sudsy water all over the place, Lindsey grabs a towel. Her hands look wizened and old. That's just the cost of staying clean. And she needs to stay clean now more than ever.

Since Christmas, Lindsey has been watching, with growing anxiety, the spread of the coronavirus throughout the world. She's just read that a second case has been discovered in the Republic of Ireland. There's at least one case in Northern Ireland too. Her parents tell her not to worry about it, but she's decided to be especially careful.

As she dries her hands, she hears a shout. She squints out the window and sees a man climb up onto the wall at the end of the garden.

Oh my god. A burglar?

She kills the light in the kitchen so she can see better. After a moment, her eyes adjust. Now two men are perched on the wall, like a couple of pigeons. The searchlight passes over the men, lighting them up. They're kitted out in black body armour and black baseball caps, and each of them holds a machine gun.

Lindsey gapes. Is she really seeing what she thinks she's seeing?

Terrorists?

A third man pulls himself up on the wall, slings his machine gun around to the front, and points it around the garden.

No, not terrorists, Lindsey thinks.

These men look like part of the Emergency Response Unit, a specialist armed division of the Gardaí, the Irish police. The ones who deal with dangerous situations, where there might be an immediate threat of violence.

Lindsey knows a little about the ERU. Katherine Dunne, a friend and fellow student in Lindsey's Modern Irish History module, has decided that she wants to be a Garda instead of a historian. She talks endlessly about the merits of the different divisions within the force – which ones wear a uniform, which ones carry a gun, how the different kinds of officers spend their time.

The more Lindsey looks, the more certain she is that the men on the wall are part of an ERU team.

Their presence here is completely surreal.

It's also terrifying.

Lindsey's stomach churns. She takes a long breath, trying to control herself. Her mood is already foul. Her parents are visiting from Aberdeen, and they've been heaping pressure on her to arrange a meeting with Adrian Connolly.

"We need to *talk* to this boy," Dad said.

Although Lindsey doesn't agree, she's called Adrian a dozen times and tried to persuade him to come and see her. She doesn't *want* to see him, but she figures if her parents meet him once, they'll stop bugging her. Adrian is full of excuses. Humiliating as it is, Lindsey realises that he'd rather play computer games than visit her.

Adrian is in Lindsey's Mediaeval Europe module. Lindsey did pretty well in first and second year, her love of history making the Bachelor of Arts a pleasure. Now, in her third year, things are trickier. Meanwhile, Adrian has struggled with his grades since day one.

A noise downstairs makes Lindsey freeze.

There's a thud.

A bang.

Then footsteps.

Someone pounding up the stairs.

Lindsey walks over to the door. It has no peephole, so she can't tell what was happening, but she knows someone is getting closer.

They're just outside.

Suddenly there's a bang on the door.

She holds her breath, hoping the person will go away.

Bang, bang, bang.

"Hello?" Lindsey calls.

A man shouts, "Gardaí. Open up."
What did they want with her?
"Is it – am I—"
"Open up *now*."
Lindsey swallows, and unlocks her door.

CHAPTER THREE

The man at Lindsey's door isn't kitted out in SWAT gear like the people in the garden, but in a black hoodie and dark jeans. His short hair is thick and fluffy. He looks a little older than Lindsey, though thick stubble makes his precise age hard to pinpoint.

He says, "Detective Garda. I need to come into your home."

The man sounds out of breath, like he's been running. Lindsey looks at him. Is he really a detective? She knows they're plain-clothes officers – so she can't expect him to wear a uniform – but she expects a suit. At least, a shirt and tie.

On the other hand, she's seen photos of officers on the news, and some of them look as scruffy as the criminals they're after.

Undercover officers, maybe.

She wonders if that's the situation here. Are her neighbours drug dealers? She can't believe anyone in her building would get involved in such a thing. They seem like nice people, mostly young professionals and other college students.

Lindsey decides she wanted to see some ID.

She says, "Do you have—"

"Sorry, no time."

Lindsey gasps as the man pushes past her. He wafts a rank smell of sweat as he goes by.

Now he's inside her small apartment. The door opens out into the sitting room, which is combined with a kitchen area at the other end of the room. Two doorways lead to the apartment's other rooms: the bathroom and the bedroom.

The man strides to the window and looks out. He steps back at once, cursing under his breath.

A feeling of vertigo hits Lindsey.

Something's wrong.

She gazes at the open doorway. Some primal part of her brain screams at her to run through it.

"Hey, hey, hey," the man says. He's watching Lindsey. "Close the door for a minute."

"What's going on?" Lindsey asks.

"Tell me your name."

"Lindsey."

"Okay, Lindsey. I'm Dean. I'm here to help, alright? I want you to close the door and step inside."

"Why—"

"I'll explain everything, but I need your co-operation, Lindsey. It's important. Please do it now."

There are more footsteps downstairs, coming from the back. The communal laundry facilities are housed in a shed in the garden. Usually the back door of the house is left unlocked so people can come and go as they do their washing. This arrangement has never caused a problem before. Not while Lindsey has lived here. After all, this is a nice area, and the garden is secure. No one is going to wander in.

But now men are swarming around the property, Lindsey thinks, so it must not be as secure as she believed.

Oh god, oh god, oh god.

She tastes the carbonara sauce rising in her throat. She forces it back down again.

"Close the door," Dean says. "And step away from it."

His voice has gone cold.

Lindsey hears heavy footsteps downstairs. Moving fast. The Emergency Response Unit is coming. But no one is in sight yet.

"This is the last time I'm going to ask," Dean says.

He lifts his T-shirt and pulls a gun from the waistband of his jeans. He points it straight at Lindsey's heart.

"Oh, god help me," Lindsey says.

"Take it easy," Dean says. "All you have to do is close the door."

A burst of static comes from a walkie-talkie downstairs. Then a distorted voice, like an announcement over an airport PA system. Lindsey is never able to make out what's said over those things. She only catches the words, "have visual... bike... headed north..."

The men move away.

The sound fades.

Lindsey closes the door and turns to the man with the gun. She knows she's blown it. That was her chance to escape.

CHAPTER FOUR

Lindsey stares at the gun in the man's hand. Dean – that's his name. She presumes it's a fake name. Why would he tell her the real one?

"Sit down," he says.

He unzips his hoodie, revealing a blood-spattered white T-shirt. His face is hard to read. Does he look like a bad person? The kind who'd shoot her? What did that even look like?

Lindsey says, "Please don't hurt me."

"I won't, unless you make me. Now sit down."

Reluctantly, she moves away from the door. The couch is pressed against the side wall, halfway between the door and the kitchenette. Lindsey lowers herself into the couch, never taking her eyes off Dean's gun.

Most evenings, Lindsey studies at the small desk set up opposite the couch. When she isn't studying, she lies on the couch and watches Netflix on her laptop.

Dean pulls the swivel chair away from the desk and rotates it. He swings a leg over and sits down. The gun rests casually in his right hand. It's pointed at the floor but that could change any time.

"I want you to listen carefully," Dean says.

"Alright."

"I'm going to call someone. He's going to come and get me."

"Okay, sure."

"You and I are going to sit here and wait for my friend. When he gets here, I'm going to leave with him."

"Okay. Yeah, okay."

"You cause me any trouble," Dean says, "and you're going to be dead when I leave."

Lindsey's stomach dives. It feels like she's on a roller-coaster. That moment when the train begins to hurtle downwards.

"Oh god—"

Dean says, "Annoying me counts as trouble."

Lindsey shuts her mouth.

It's going to be alright. If she cooperates, everything will be okay.

Dean is silent for a minute, his brows tightly knit as he listens. His face relaxes as the sound of helicopter blades begins to fade.

Lindsey jumps when her phone rings in her jeans pocket. Dean holds out his hand. She gives him the phone and he looks at the screen.

"Who's Adrian?" Dean asks.

"He's my – my boyfriend. Or something. I – I don't know."

Dean has thin lips, the same colour as the rest of his face. Now those lips twist at the corners. Dean points at the vase of pink tulips by the window.

"Oh, so that's who gave you those flowers."

"No," Lindsey says in a small voice. The only thing Adrian ever gave her was a heap of trouble. Dean raises his eyebrows.

"What does Adrian want?" he asks.

"I don't know."

"Never mind."

He swivels the chair around and sets Lindsey's phone down on the desk, then swivels back to face Lindsey and takes out his own phone. He dials a number and watches Lindsey while it rings.

"Hey, it's me," he says.

Lindsey strains to hear both sides of the conversation. Then she thinks maybe it's best if she doesn't know what's said.

"I need you to pick me up." Dean says. He listens. When he talks again, he's shouting. "I know that. I need you to come get me. There's a chopper, armed Gardaí. No, not outside, it's okay here."

Another pause. Then Dean gives Lindsey's address to the person on the other end of the line. He ends the call and puts the phone in his pocket.

He looks at her.

She looks at him.

"What did you do?" Lindsey asks.

"You don't want to know."

Dean gets to his feet and walks over to the window. He keeps low, and – when he reaches the window – he lifts his head slowly to look out.

Lindsey stares at his back.

Is he really going to let me go? she thinks. *What if he doesn't want to leave peacefully? What if he gets violent?*

Her phone sits on the desk six feet away. She can grab it, call someone. Does she have time to dial 911 and give the cops her address?

No, Lindsey, you're not in Aberdeen. Here, you call 999, and you get the Gardaí.

She leans forward.

Dean is still intent on the window. Lindsey leans forward more. Can she reach out and grab the phone? Her chest is tight, her legs like jelly. She'll need to be fast. Can she call someone before he gets to her?

Is there time?

"Don't even think about it," Dean says.

He hasn't turned. But he knows what she's thinking. Lindsey's breath quickens. It feels like there's a brass band is playing in her belly.

Dean turns away from the window. Lindsey's Mom always says the eyes are the windows to soul. She doesn't know about that, but Dean's eyes are wild.

"I told you not to cause me trouble."

Lindsey says, "I'm sorry. I didn't do anything."

"You'd turn me in, in a second, wouldn't you?" Slowly walking to the couch, Dean raises the gun. "You'd love to see me go down. I told you I'd kill you if you caused trouble."

"No, please!"

She pushes back against the couch as if trying to disappear into it, but there's nowhere to go. Dean comes closer. The gun barrel all she can see.

"You're all the same," Dean says.

She's about to die. Lindsey knows it. She shields her face with her hands, though it's futile.

Dean takes aim.

This is when the baby starts crying.

CHAPTER FIVE

Lindsey has called Adrian Connolly three times today. The third time, he's eating a Hawaiian pizza in his kitchen, and he smears melted cheese and tomato sauce all over the screen of his Samsung when he answers.

He picks up, though.

Adrian's flat mate, Pete, is sitting at the kitchen table, eating a microwave curry. He watches Adrian take the call. Adrian speaks to Lindsey for a few minutes. Or rather, Adrian listens. He keeps things non-committal and gets off the line as soon as he can.

"Bullshit," Adrian says, after hanging up.

Pete laughs. "What did she say?"

"Same rubbish. Wants us to talk."

"You better go see her," Pete says. "You've got a child together."

"No way."

"Did you break up with her?"

"No, because, like, we were never really together."

"Does Lindsey know that?"

Adrian shrugs.

"Fuckin' father of the year." Pete says. "I can't believe she got together with you."

They both laugh.

Home is a four-bed apartment Adrian shares with Pete and two other students. The place is a bit grubby – the shower stall that's meant to be white is stained nuclear-waste green – but Adrian can't afford anything nicer, and the location is within cycling distance of college.

The building isn't far from Lindsey's place, and she keeps asking why he doesn't visit her.

For months, she didn't talk to him, and now she wants him again.

Crazy or what?

Adrian's flatmates roll their eyes whenever his phone rings, because it's *always* Lindsey. She doesn't shout at him. Instead, she asks him questions in that passive-aggressive style she's perfected.

You don't have time to visit this week, right?
You must be so busy studying, right?

Adrian finishes his pizza, throws his plate into the dishwasher.

You want to see your kid, right?

"Come on, man," Pete says, throwing his hands in the air.

"What?"

"Why can't you ever rinse a plate? You're going to break the dishwasher."

Adrian scowls. "Why would I wash the plate before it goes into the machine? The whole point of the dishwasher is to clean stuff."

He slams the door of the dishwasher shut and walks out of the kitchen before Pete can reply.

Why is everyone always on his case?

People are such jerks.

Fine, maybe he will visit Lindsey for a few minutes. Get it out of the way. Then he'll be able to relax for the rest of the evening and enjoy himself. Pick up a sixer of beer and play the PlayStation all night.

And put the baby out of his mind for good.

Adrian grabs his jacket and heads for the door. As he walks up the road, he rings Lindsey to let her know he's coming. She doesn't answer so he sends her a text message.

CHAPTER SIX

The baby is awake. The baby is crying. Lindsey holds her breath as the sound carries from the bedroom.

Dean's face darkens. He says, "Are you kidding me?"

"She'll stop soon," Lindsey says, though she has no idea if that's true. At one month old, Jazz is hardly predictable. "Really, she'll stop soon."

Maybe.

Maybe not.

Please don't kill us.

Dean cocks his head and listens to the crying, which Lindsey thought was so cute when she heard it for the first time. She was amazed that this little pink creature had come out of her. It's still hard to get her head around it, but these days she has less time to be philosophical.

Dean bends his arm, so that the gun points at the ceiling instead of Lindsey. A relief, as long as the crying doesn't make him mad.

It's impossible to explain the overwhelming sense of love – and now fear – which Lindsey feels for the child in the next room, despite the exhaustion Jazz has brought.

No one thinks Jazz is a good name – not Lindsey's parents, not Lindsey's friends – but that's what she chose anyway. It's one of the few rebellions Lindsey has made in her life.

Another is leaving Aberdeen.

Lindsey never went through the wild teenager phase that her friends enjoyed. She didn't drink, smoke or do drugs. But at eighteen, she decided to leave her home town and go to Ireland to attend college. Even her Irish-American parents were baffled, but it made sense to Lindsey. She has dual citizenship and always loved stories about Ireland. From the age of thirteen, she has read Irish poetry before bed each night. She particularly liked Patrick Kavanagh's work. And now here she is, in Kavanagh's old neighbourhood, near Dublin's Grand Canal. After two and a half years here, she feels like a local.

People say Dublin is small. But when Lindsey arrived, the city seemed big to her. Bustling, but friendly. She likes the pubs – where she drinks Coke – the traditional music, the old buildings, the weird, unplanned layout of the city, and the sense of history in every street. Trinity College was founded in 1592, making it hundreds of years older than Aberdeen. Lindsey loves that connection with the past.

Getting pregnant wasn't an act of rebellion.

That just happened.

Funny how people always gravitate towards the same part of the lecture hall. Last year, Adrian Connolly always sat one row behind Lindsey, and two seats to the left, in the Medieval Europe lectures they shared. Lindsey thought it was cute the way his lank hair always fell in his eyes.

One day, at the very start of their second year, he asked to borrow her phone charger. An after-class cappuccino at a café was his way of saying thanks.

"Where are you from?" he asked. She was impressed that he'd heard of Aberdeen.

"That's where Kurt Cobain was born, right?" Adrian said.

Lindsey began to wonder if she had finally found someone special. She thought Adrian's carefree manner hid the depths of a sensitive soul. But he wasn't so gentle in the end, and these days, his depths look more and more like shallows.

In the bedroom, Jazz continues crying.

"You better shut that baby up," Dean says.

"Yeah," Lindsey says. "I will."

"Do it."

She gets to her feet and goes into the bedroom. Jazz is moving around in the crib. Her face is bright pink, and she's waving her tiny hands.

Lindsey picks Jazz up and holds the child to her heart. The baby is more work than Lindsey ever would have thought. She needs constant attention of one sort or another, whether it's being fed, having her diaper changed, or being rocked to sleep.

Despite all the sleepless nights, the exhaustion, expense and disruption, Lindsey is glad she went through with the pregnancy. Katherine, the friend and classmate who wants to work in law enforcement, suggested an abortion. Lindsey thought about it. Looking at Jazz's scrunched-up face, Lindsey cannot imagine life without her.

Dean says, "Shut her up, will you?"

He's right behind her, in the doorway.

"I'm trying."

"Hurry up then."

"It would help if you keep your voice down."

Lindsey gasps as Dean takes her chin in his hand. Turning her face towards him, he squeezes it tight, and says, "Shut the baby up, or I'll do it. Believe me."

Tears come to Lindsey's eyes, because she *does* believe him. He must have done something awful to have armed Gardaí and a helicopter chasing him.

Did he kill someone?

Dean releases her and goes to stand by the kitchen window. The sky is fully dark now.

Blinking tears back, Lindsey rocks Jazz in her arms, and murmurs in her most comforting tone. After a while, the baby begins to settle.

Lindsey's phone, sitting on her desk, rings. Dean picks the phone up and looks at the screen.

"Adrian," he reads.

"I'm sorry."

Dean hits the red button to reject the call. The phone starts ringing again at once.

"Adrian," Dean says.

He rejects the call again.

Lindsey strokes Jazz's back. The baby should be tired, because she hasn't slept much today. Hopefully she'll fall asleep and this will all be over by the time she wakes up.

Lindsey's phone buzzes with a text message.

Go away, Adrian, she thinks. He usually ignores her, but now he suddenly wants to talk? He chose *this exact moment* to get interested? Of course, Lindsey did call him a few times today. She guesses the guilt-tripping is finally working. Just when she doesn't want it to.

Lindsey lowers Jazz into the crib and backs out of the bedroom, closing the door as quietly as she can.

Dean holds out her phone for her to look at.

I'm almost at your place. See you in a minute, Adrian's message says.

Dean hands her the phone. "Tell this idiot to get lost."

Lindsey nods, but her stomach begins to churn. Adrian never listens to anything she says, especially when she says, *No*.

CHAPTER SEVEN

Adrian stares at his phone in disbelief. Lindsey is refusing to take his call and hasn't replied to his text message.

He thrusts the phone into his jacket pocket and walks on, through the chilly March evening. Ballsbridge is quiet, though he hears a chopper's blades in the distance. Adrian wonders if its presence is related to the incident on the news, the thing Pete mentioned.

Some guy shot two people in South Dublin. The details are sketchy. Pete didn't say who the guy shot or why, just that the Gardaí are pursuing him.

Adrian shivers.

He's tempted to go home, but Lindsey's building is just ahead, so he might as well go there and get this conversation out of the way.

Plus, he doesn't like being ignored.

Who does she think she is?

Adrian's Mum calls Lindsey a "scheming Yankee slut". It's a pity his Mum knows about the baby – Adrian wouldn't have told her anything, but his sister spilled the beans. Anyway, his Mum is right. Lindsey seduced him. She wanted a baby and used him to get it. Now she probably wants him to pay for it. That's why she's been calling him since the baby was born. She's found out how expensive a kid is.

That day Lindsey and Adrian got together, he wanted to thank her for letting him borrow her phone charger during class. That was it. But she roped him into buying her an overpriced cappuccino and flashed her eyelids at him while she talked to him in her American accent.

"Say again?" is Lindsey's favourite phrase. She said that when he invited her back to his place, and, again later, when he took her to his bedroom and got her on the bed. She pretended to have second thoughts after they'd been making out for ten minutes. Well, that was bullshit. She knew what she was getting into.

Half-digested pizza sloshes around in a sea of Pepsi in Adrian's stomach.

A man coughs as he walks past. Adrian wonders if he has that virus. A lot of people are infected now, but mostly in other countries. People say it's just a bad flu. Only old or weak people need to be worried. Adrian is fine. He's going to be alright.

He's young and strong.

Also, he's angry.

Lindsey misled him. Adrian assumed she was on the pill, and she didn't tell him different. Not his fault she got pregnant. Clearly getting knocked up *was* her plan. She used Adrian as a sperm donor.

He checks his phone, but she still hasn't replied.

"Bitch," he says, and puts the phone back into his pocket. "Scheming Yankee slut."

She's probably in a bad mood with him because he hasn't gone to see her since she gave birth. February was a busy month for Adrian.

He was sick one week and another week, he was in Amsterdam with friends. That was a wild time. When he came home, it took three days to recover from the hangover. Not that he expected any sympathy, but he wasn't going to change his whole life because of one stray sperm cell.

Sorry, but I didn't have parenting in my study planner, he thinks.

If Lindsey wants to become a mother, fine, good for her, enjoy it – but Adrian has no interest in being a dad. At twenty-one, his own life has barely started.

Well, now he's going to tell her he wants nothing to do with the baby, and that he never wants to talk to her again. That she should stop ringing him.

The thought of getting rid of her makes him smile.

Lindsey's place comes into view – one of those old Georgian buildings, subdivided by the landlord. Adrian has never been inside, but he passes it every day.

"Scheming Yankee bitch slut," he says.

He walks up the driveway and climbs the steps to her door. He presses her buzzer and holds it down for a long time.

CHAPTER EIGHT

Lindsey stares at the message on her phone.

I'm almost at your place. See you in a minute.

It's just like Adrian to make things worse than they already are. Lindsey's hands are damp with sweat. Adrian won't listen to her. She knows he won't. He never has, ever since they met. He did what he wanted and left her to clean up afterwards.

Now she has another selfish man by her side. But this one has a gun in his hand, and she thinks he's willing to use it.

"Call him," Dean says. "Tell him to go away. Don't say anything about me."

"Okay," Lindsey replies.

Dean opens the door to Lindsey's bedroom and stands next to the crib, looking down at Jazz.

He doesn't need to say anything.

Lindsey has butterflies in her chest, and not the good kind. The sickening flutter of nerves. The baby didn't even exist one short month earlier, yet now

Lindsey feels her life only matters insofar as it means protecting her baby girl. She doesn't know where this loves comes from, but it's undeniable.

She presses the green button on the phone to call Adrian, just as the intercom buzzes. Its shrill tone makes her jump.

Adrian.

He's already here. He leaves his finger on the buzzer for ages, the grating noise filling the whole apartment.

Lindsey thinks, *He's going to wake Jazz again.*

Maybe she's already awake. Lindsey glances behind her. Dean hasn't shifted, but his lips are pressed tight together. He looks dangerously close to snapping.

The intercom panel is set into the wall next to the door. The button on the panel releases the lock on the front door of the building. There's no camera and the sound on the intercom is broken, so there's no way of checking who's outside. The only choice is to unlock the door or not.

Right now, Lindsey is most certainly not going to open it.

She's still calling Adrian on her phone. Finally, he answers.

"Yeah?"

"Adrian, hi."

"I'm outside, Lindsey. Open the door."

She says, "Look, I'm sorry but this is really not a good time."

"You wanted me to come and I came all this way."

Despite herself, Lindsey feels a pulse of irritation. She said, "You came half a kilometre? Big deal."

"I didn't plan to go out," Adrian says. "I was studying all day."

"I bet."

"Open the door, Lindsey."

The buzzer sounds again, then stops. Sounds again, then stops again.

Lindsey always found the buzzer annoyingly loud. But her life never depended on it before.

"Adrian, quit it."

"So let me in. I want to talk about us."

"Forget us," Lindsey says.

"You're dumping me?" Adrian's voice is furious. "*You* are dumping *me*? Open the fucking door."

Lindsey is so taken aback that she holds the phone away from her ear for a moment. Where's that anger coming from? What has she ever done to him?

A gurgle comes from the bedroom. Dean is still standing next to the crib, but he's watching Lindsey.

Lindsey tries to keep her voice calm. She says into the phone, "It's not the right time to talk, okay? Maybe later."

"Fine," Adrian says. "I'll press *all* the buzzers. Someone will open this door."

"No, don't do that!"

But he does. She hears the muffled sound of the buzzer sounding in the nearby apartments. Lindsey wonders if anyone is expecting a visitor or has ordered a takeaway.

She hopes not.

"Alright," Adrian says. "That was easy. I guess not everyone in this building is as uptight as you. I'm in."

CHAPTER NINE

Karl has been pedalling hard since his encounter with the man in the lane. He's moving towards the city centre at a pretty fast clip. That guy looked like trouble, but it's none of Karl's business.

The eighty euro is welcome, as Karl is broke. He figures he'll pick up some new runners with the money, maybe a new hoodie. The hoodie the man took was Karl's favourite, but it was cheap, and Karl can replace it. In fact, he needs to, or else his parents will ask a lot of questions.

The helicopter Karl heard earlier is coming closer. Sirens are coming closer too.

Looking for me?

The man is on the run. That's clear. He wouldn't last long wearing the fluorescent orange jacket he had on earlier, the one Karl now wears. Karl decides to ditch it.

He reaches the south side of Stephen's Green. He eases his bike to a stop next to a bin. As he scrambles to get the jacket off, the helicopter roars closer, and hovers directly overhead. A thick beam of light envelopes Karl, completely blinding him. Disoriented, he loses balance and tumbles onto the footpath.

A voice blares over a loudspeaker.

"This is the Gardaí. Do not move."

The words are almost drowned out by sirens.

A patrol car screams to a stop at the side of the road. Karl squints as two officers jump out.

A van screams to a halt next to the car and what looks like a SWAT team swarms out of the back, with machine guns aimed at Karl.

"Don't move," a man shouts. "Hands in the air."

Karl couldn't move if he wanted to. He's frozen with fear. The only part not frozen is his bladder, which he feels emptying down his pants leg. It's all very well to see an arrest on TV. It's completely different in real life, when all those guns, all that shouting, is directed at you.

While one gunman keeps his weapon trained on Karl, another runs over and grabs him by the scruff of the neck.

A slim woman in body armour comes over. Despite her size, she's clearly in charge. She brushes a strand of red hair out of her eyes and looks Karl in the face.

"It's not Cullen," she shouts. "It's just some gobshite."

"I – I'm sorry," Karl says.

"Shut up." The woman gets in Karl's face and says, "Where is he?"

CHAPTER TEN

Dean presses the side of the Makarov to his temple. He has a pounding headache, and the gun's cool, black steel gives him a moment's relief. He squeezes his eyes shut for a second, then goes over to where Lindsey is standing, next to the intercom.

Her boyfriend is coming up the stairs.

All Dean wanted was to hide out for a few minutes. Why does nothing ever go right?

The apartment has no other exit. Just one door, and the window is too small to squeeze through. He'll just have to deal with this situation.

Lindsey is watching him warily.

She says, "I can go outside and talk to Adrian."

"And tell him that you're being held hostage? I don't think so."

"I won't say anything."

"No," Dean says. "You can tell him from here."

He's not going back to jail. He's only enjoyed three days of freedom since walking through the gates of Mountjoy Prison. And *enjoyed* isn't the right word. It's been a nightmare.

The footsteps outside the apartment draw closer.

"Lindsey? Let me in."

The guy has a reedy, nasal voice. It sounds like his nose is blocked.

Bang, bang, bang.

Lindsey jumps as the guy's fist hits the other side of the door. She takes a breath, then calls out, "I told you, it's not a good time."

"What are you doing in there?"

"Nothing, Adrian. But Jazz is sleeping."

"You got a guy in there?" he asks.

"No. It's just me and Jazz."

"Then let me see you. I'm not going anywhere until you let me in."

The guy bangs on the door again. He's going to alert the whole building that something is up. Dean needs to get rid of him fast.

What if he does let the guy into the apartment?

The place is tiny. There's nowhere to hide in the main room, the combined sitting room and kitchen. That only leaves the bathroom and the bedroom. If Adrian wants to see the baby, Dean can hide in the bathroom. Maybe he can even slip out of the apartment while the lovebirds *ooh* and *aah* over the kid.

Or else he can go into the bedroom. Being near the baby would be better in terms of leverage. It means Lindsey won't try anything. He can hide in the wardrobe and he'll hear everything Lindsey says.

"Don't make me mad, Lindsey," Adrian shouts.

Lindsey shakes her head slightly. She whispers to Dean, "What should I do?"

Dean wipes his face with the crook of his elbow.

"I'll hide," he says. "Let him in for a minute. Then get him out of here. Don't do anything stupid. Think of your baby."

She nods.

"Hang on," Lindsey calls out to Adrian. "I'm opening the door."

Dean goes to the bedroom. The baby is asleep and thank goodness for that. He opens the wardrobe, but there's no room for him to fit inside.

The only place to hide is under the bed. He lies on his belly and crawls underneath it. There's just enough for him to fit. It's dark, and there's a faintly musty smell. His movements stir up some dust, and it's all he can do to stop himself sneezing. He turns his head and sees the base of the crib nearby.

Sleep, baby, sleep.

Lindsey opens the door.

CHAPTER ELEVEN

Sirens screaming, lights flashing, the three vehicles tear down Leeson Street. Motorists move aside. People on the footpath stop and stare.

Detective Sergeant Irene Flaherty is in the lead car, an unmarked BMW 3 Series, but a patrol car and a van are right behind her. All of them are moving fast.

For five years, she's been attached to the Emergency Response Unit, part of the Special Tactics & Operations Command. The high-octane work suits her, as she gets bored easily. Just ask her ex-husband.

Flaherty is in charge here.

Which means she's to blame if Cullen gets away.

Grinding her teeth, she stares at the road ahead and urges the car to move faster. She feels like an idiot. They were right behind Cullen in that lane. With that stupid jacket, he basically had a *shoot me* sign on his back.

Yet, somehow, he disappeared – and found a decoy to lead them astray.

The AgustaWestland AW139 twin-engine helicopter races ahead of them through the night sky. It will get to the area first and scout around with its searchlight. Cullen is dangerous. Flaherty knows that. He's also armed and desperate. It's a hell of a combination.

She can't let him get away.

Flaherty makes another call.

"Get the dogs," she says.

CHAPTER TWELVE

Lindsey opens the door and finds Adrian standing in the hall. The bare bulb hanging from the ceiling doesn't do his looks any favours. Lindsey wonders how she was ever attracted to him.

She used to be intrigued by his pink cheeks, long black eyelashes, and messy hair. Together with his droopy eyelids, she thought his features made him look like a sleepy intellectual. Now, not so much.

"About time," Adrian says, and brushes past her.

Lindsey closes the door.

Adrian is here, in her home… She's imagined this situation many times.

She was so upset after their night together that she never wanted to see him again, never wanted to see anyone again. When they were kissing in Adrian's bedroom, things were fine. Lindsey still had a pleasant alcohol buzz at that time. They had visited a pub after the café. Unused to drinking, two gin-and-tonics went straight to her head.

She barely remembers the taxi to Adrian's apartment. Just remembers laughing a lot. And the driver's face in the rear-view mirror. He tried to cheat them out of their change because he could see they were drunk. Adrian was alert enough to argue with him.

They went into Adrian's apartment. They kissed. Adrian made her a cocktail. They kissed some more. They moved to his bedroom and things got heavier. She was lying on his bed, starting to feel sick when he began to undress her.

Lindsey asked him to stop, to slow down, *please*. He didn't. He pinned her arms to the bed. The feeling of powerlessness was terrifying.

Like a nightmare.

Like vertigo.

As she hurried home that night, Lindsey wondered if she had led Adrian on. Or maybe it was a misunderstanding, something to do with a culture gap?

Was it her fault?

Lindsey didn't know what to think, and she had no one to ask. She stopped at the side of the road and vomited, then walked home feeling more miserable than she ever had in her life.

The taste of self-disgust had hardly left her mouth since. It grew as Lindsey's parents digested the news that she was pregnant. They had questions.

Who's the father? What's he like? Do you love him?

Does he love you?

They're Catholics and they believe in marriage. So does Lindsey, but not with Adrian.

After months of avoiding him, then hounding him, he's finally in her apartment.

"Well, where's the kid?" Adrian asks. He takes off his jacket and flings it on the couch, as if he's in his own home.

"Asleep," Lindsey says. "I'll show you."

Adrian's nose wrinkles. "This place stinks. Were you working out?"

He's right. The smell of Dean's sweat hangs in the air. A rank, masculine odour.

"Um, yeah. Sorry."

He follows her into her bedroom. Dean has left the door open. He must be under the bed, as that's the only hiding place.

It's weird to have Adrian so close to her, and she doesn't like it.

After she found out she was pregnant, she started sitting in a different part of the lecture hall from usual. She made sure to arrive late and leave early, and generally kept away from Adrian.

Her parents insisted that she tell him she was pregnant. Mom and Dad didn't know he'd forced himself on her, if that was what had happened, and Lindsey was still trying to figure that out. For some reason, she felt like she didn't have the right to make that accusation. Because what if she was wrong? Most of the night is a blur.

Lindsey's parents think Adrian must be a nice kid if Lindsey would choose him. She hasn't the heart to tell them she made a terrible choice. That the guy isn't boyfriend material, never mind father material.

Right now, Mom and Dad are at a hotel a mile away. They came to Dublin to see her through the birth. Their plan is to stay in Dublin for another three weeks before returning home. They're working hard to persuade Lindsey to go with them.

Tempting idea.

Adrian has ruined Ireland for her. But Lindsey is afraid if she starts running from trouble now, she might never stop.

She takes a steadying breath, walks around the side of the crib and watches Adrian approach. His face is as blank as an insect's. He looks down at the baby, then up at Lindsey.

"Wow," he laughs. "A real baby. Are you going to keep it?"

CHAPTER THIRTEEN

Stopped at a red light, Michael Kilpatrick grips the steering wheel so hard his fingers turn white. Under his jumper, his T-shirt is drenched in cold sweat and the skin on his scalp prickles as if he has a fever.

What if he *does* have a fever? That Covid-19 shit?

But Michael has bigger problems than the virus. He takes one hand off the wheel and runs his fingers over his bald head. Everything has gone to hell, and now he's making things worse. He wipes the sweat off his upper lip and tries to think.

It should have been a simple job. Holding up a cash-in-transit van in Ballsbridge. Getting away with thousands in cash. Just him and Dean. A couple of handguns. A couple of balaclavas. What could go wrong?

Michael watched the vans for weeks, getting used to their routine. It's not rocket science. He had a plan and it would have worked if Dean hadn't got distracted. Dean didn't even make it to the rendezvous. On the way to do the job, he went to see his wife.

Look how that turned out.

Michael heard about it on the news. Of course, he had to abandon the plan. And then he got the call.

I need you to pick me up.

He's known Dean a long time. He knows Dean's wife too. *Knew* her, at least. She was seeing another guy while Dean was in jail for the last job. Everyone on the street knew about it. Dean was inside for two years, after all, and that's a long time. Michael visited him a couple of times, but never said anything. Not after Dean boasted that his wife never missed her weekly visit.

The light changes to green and Michael hits the accelerator hard, passing the U.S embassy, heading towards the address Dean gave him.

Michael should *not* be doing this, not even for an old pal.

A bright red Lexus cuts him off at the next junction. Michael swears, then watches as the Lexus drives along in front of him until they both stop at the next set of lights.

Michael rolls down his window and shouts, "Hey asshole, go fuck yourself."

Straight away, the driver's door opens, and a guy gets out. A big guy, with square shoulders and arms like the trunk of an oak tree. He's wearing an XL suit, looks like a former rugby player. The guy walks towards Michael's car.

There's confidence in that walk.

Overconfidence.

"What the fuck?" Michael mutters.

He doesn't want this guy coming over to his window, towering over him. So Michael gets out of his car.

The guy is a couple of metres away.

"What did you say to me?" the big guy asks.

Michael says, "Piss off."

The guy smiles.

"That's not what you said."

Maybe he's the type that wants a fight. A gym-rat with no outlet for the kind of high-grade aggression that the treadmill can't relieve. All that muscle going to waste. Maybe he had a hard day at the office. Who knows? That's not Michael's problem, unless the guy makes it his problem.

"Get back in your piece-of-shit car and go away," Michael says. He's aware that he's like a midget next to the other man. Small and skeletal, with a bald head. No fat to cushion a blow. No muscle to return one.

But he does have one thing.

As the guy comes within striking distance, Michael pulls the Makarov from the back of his pants. He waves the pistol in the guy's face.

The guy stops. Michael can see his shock for a second before he recovers his composure. The big guy smiles again.

"Where'd you find that? A toy shop?"

He tenses his arms, takes another step closer.

The point of no return.

Michael shoots him in the centre of that big muscular chest. The guy hits the ground a second later. His eyes are wide. There's a hole in his shirt. Blood pumping onto the tarmac.

Michael shoots him again in the chest, then once in the head.

The guy is definitely dead.

Michael looks around, sees another car approaching. An SUV. The car slows as it approaches. The passenger window powers down.

The driver is alone in the car. He leans over the passenger seat and says, "What the—"

Michael puts a bullet between his eyes. Dead at once, he slumps against the driver's side window. The SUV eases to a stop after a few metres.

"Shit," Michael says.

He gets back in his car. Drives around the XL corpse. Drives around the SUV.

Michael checks the address Dean gave him one more time. He has to pick up Dean and get them both away from here fast. He won't hesitate to use the Makarov again if anyone gets in his way.

There can be no witnesses.

CHAPTER FOURTEEN

Lindsey's bed is pressed into the corner of the room. There's a small window on the side wall, with a nice view of the adjacent building's brickwork. A wardrobe takes up the wall at the foot of the bed, every cubic inch of it occupied by Lindsey's clothes and shoes.

The crib is squeezed in beside the bed. Lindsey's Dad insisted on putting the flat pack together for her, perhaps as an excuse to spend time with Lindsey. She enjoyed the time together, but he bugged her by mentioning Adrian all the time.

She wonders if returning to Aberdeen is the best thing to do. Maybe she'd appreciate small-town life more now.

If she ever gets out of this mess.

Adrian stands at the foot of the crib and peers down into it. Dean must be under her bed. Lindsey is gripped by the irrational fear that he'll reach out and grab her ankle. Pull her under the bed like some horror-movie monster.

Dean's sweat hangs in the air even more strongly here. She can tell Adrian smells it too, judging by the way he wrinkles his nose.

"Have a shower, why don't you?"

Lindsey frowns. "What did you say?"

"I said, have a shower."

"Shh," she whispers, "Keep it down or you'll wake Jazz. No, I mean, what did you say before that?"

"I asked if you're going to keep it."

"Right." So Lindsey heard him correctly. "As you can see, it's a bit late to get an abortion."

Adrian doesn't smile.

"Aren't you going to give it up for adoption?"

"*Her*," Lindsey says.

"What?"

"Jazz is a girl."

Adrian nods distractedly. "Right. What a name. Do you not like Blues? Or Rock?"

Lindsey flushes but says nothing. Jazz was meant to evoke a spirit of freedom. Of self-determination. But maybe it's silly.

No.

She can't change her mind about something just because Adrian disagrees with her. Everyone is entitled to think their own thoughts, right?

Adrian reaches down and squeezes Jazz's leg.

"Hmm," he says. "You know it doesn't look like me. I don't think it's mine. My family is famous for having excellent reflexes, even as babies."

"Say again?"

Adrian points to Jazz. "I'm pretty sure it isn't mine."

"*She. She* isn't yours – and of course she is." Lindsey says it through gritted teeth. She can't believe Adrian.

"It. She. Whatever."

"Let's go back to the kitchen," Lindsey whispers.

Adrian walks out first. Lindsey doesn't think Dean will be pleased if she closes the bedroom door, so she leaves it open.

Adrian stands by the sink, looking out the window.

Has it really only been a few minutes since Lindsey saw the Emergency Response Unit outside, their machine guns gleaming under the light of a search helicopter?

Folding her arms, Lindsey stands in the middle of the room.

Go, she thinks. *Just go. Please.*

Adrian turns to her. "If you're looking for money," he says, "you're out of luck. I'm not paying for the kid. I didn't ask for it."

"Fine."

As if she thinks this dummy has any money.

Adrian says, "That's what I came here to say. I didn't want this thing."

"Fine. You can go now."

Adrian's face darkens. "You phoned me and texted me a million times, Lindsey. You wanted to talk. Now I'm here and all you say is *fine*?"

She doesn't answer. What is there to say?

Adrian smiles. "Maybe you called for something else? Maybe you missed me?"

"Ugh."

"We've already gone to bed together. You know, it doesn't make any difference if we do it again."

"I'd like you to leave now. Please leave."

Adrian doesn't move.

CHAPTER FIFTEEN

The BMW 3 Series screeches to a halt at the end of the lane. The last known location of Dean Cullen.

Detective Sergeant Irene Flaherty steps out of the car. Her men swarm out of their vehicles, tooling up with Heckler & Kochs. The Emergency Response Unit uses the HK416 A5 assault rifle. Good German engineering that will stop Dean Cullen fast, assuming they can find him.

"Spread out," Flaherty says to two groups of officers. "He can't have gone far."

The third group of men stands next to her, waiting for instructions.

For a second, she's blinded by the searchlight from the AW139 helicopter as it passes overhead.

She opens the back door of her car.

"Get out," she tells the kid. Karl is young and scared, but Flaherty doesn't feel much sympathy. He knows what he did was wrong. Leading them on a wild goose chase. "Show me where you encountered Cullen," she says.

He nods and walks down the lane. Flaherty follows, and the men follow Flaherty.

The lane is lined with stone walls. Karl stops in front of a wooden door set into a wall.

"This is where I came out of my garden," Karl says.

"Tell me again."

"I wheeled my bike out here," Karl says. "I was about to cycle to my friend's house. And I heard the guy shouting. He wanted my hoodie."

"Not your bike?"

"No. We swapped, my hoodie for his jacket."

Flaherty nods.

Dean Cullen didn't want to get away faster. If he did, he would have taken the bike. His strategy must be the opposite of that – to stay here and let the Flaherty and her men go away. Which they did, to chase Karl.

She wonders if Dean Cullen is still nearby.

They weren't gone long.

He might have slipped away already, but how? Reports said he was blood-spattered and carrying a weapon. He would hardly get on a bus. But maybe he stole a car.

Or else he's still here.

Trying to wait them out.

Flaherty looks around, wondering where she'd go if she was on the run.

She dismisses Karl and waits for the dog handler to arrive. Dean's jacket will provide a scent.

CHAPTER SIXTEEN

Dean lies under the bed and listens to Lindsey and Adrian's conversation. Listens closely for any sign she's trying to warn her boyfriend that Dean is there.

The moron sounds completely oblivious.

And he isn't leaving.

By now, the dust under the bed has settled, but tiny motes still tickle the hair in Dean's nostrils. Through sheer willpower, he forces himself not to sneeze.

He can't afford to be found out.

Or can he?

Dean is wanted in connection with two deaths. It occurs to him that it makes little difference now if he commits any more crimes. If he gets caught, he'll go away for a long time anyway. Forever, probably.

He'll make sure he isn't caught. He'll do whatever he needs to do.

The Gardaí have moved off, but they might come back any time. They'll bring reinforcements. More men and more guns.

He hopes Michael is nearly here. Michael might not be a good person, but he's a good friend. Dean takes a breath and decides he'll give it one more minute. Then he'll get up, whether Adrian is gone or not.

Tightening his grip on the pistol, he prepares himself to move.

His body is coiled like a spring.

Too Tight.

CHAPTER SEVENTEEN

Lindsey feels like screaming. She's got a dangerous criminal in her home, and Adrian is trying to proposition her. Instead of slapping him, she digs her fingernails into the soft flesh of her palms.

She's asked him to leave but he's still standing in the middle of the sitting room, as if he owns the place.

Lindsey thinks of her father. Something he said, while he was putting together the crib for Jazz. "That Romeo of yours can't be so bad. After all, you like him."

But her Dad is wrong.

She doesn't like Adrian, and she's not sure she ever did. Maybe she just liked the idea of someone liking her.

"You think you're better than me," Adrian says. "Why is that?"

Lindsey is confused. "Say again?"

"Say again," Adrian echoes. "How American. You should hear what my mother calls you."

Lindsey is surprised Adrian mentioned her. "Your mother knows about me?"

"Yeah."

"Let me guess. She blames me."

Adrian waves his index finger from side to side in front of her face. "Doesn't matter what you say, Lindsey. I'm not giving you a cent."

"I don't want your money, you idiot!"

Suddenly the smile falls from Adrian's face. He hits her before she knows what's happening. Knocks her head to the side. Another bang as her head bounces off the wall. Steadying herself, she puts a hand to her cheek and looks at him. His face is dark red, like it was that night in his apartment.

He pushes her back against the wall.

"Not a cent. You hear me? That baby isn't mine."

Lindsey's natural meekness means her first thought is to assure Adrian that she really doesn't want his money. But she's a mother now. She has to be stronger than she was before.

So she knees him in the balls, and watches him double over, clasping his hands over his crotch, as a howl of pain escapes his lips.

The next logical thing would be to get away from him, but she can't. He's in her home and a wanted criminal has a gun to her baby's head.

She's not going anywhere.

Adrian needs to leave.

Lindsey opens the door to the hallway and tries to push Adrian out it.

He wobbles for a moment, then recovers, pushing back against her. As they struggle in the doorway, a phone starts ringing. An unfamiliar ringtone, coming from the bedroom.

Dean's phone.

The caller must be his friend.

Accomplice, Lindsey thinks, *not friend.*

She lets go of Adrian, but he grabs her arm and squeezes it.

"You're going to pay for that, you scheming Yankee slut."

Lindsey hears Dean answer the phone, talk quietly into it.

Adrian looks towards the bedroom. "Who's that?" he asks. "Is someone else here?"

He lets go of Lindsey when Dean emerges from the bedroom. She backs away as Dean walks past Adrian and presses the buzzer on the intercom.

Lindsey hears the front door unlock. She can see down the staircase to the front door, and she catches a glimpse of the door opening. A thin man, wearing a balaclava, steps into the hall.

Adrian is still staring at Dean. There's glee in his eyes.

"Were you hiding in the bedroom? This is your new boyfriend, Lindsey? I—"

Dean grabs Adrian by the scruff of the neck, pulls him away from the wall, then spins him around. He grabs the back of Adrian's head, and then drives it forwards, smashing his face into the wall.

Adrian crumples to the floor.

Lindsey looks down at him. She's horrified but she also feels a little satisfaction at the thought that things don't always go Adrian's way.

She doesn't get to enjoy the feeling for long because the man in the balaclava is outside the door, and he looks scarier than Dean.

CHAPTER EIGHTEEN

Dean has never been so relieved to see Michael Kilpatrick. He's a tough little guy. A fighter. And a real pro when it comes to bank jobs, breaking-and-entering, cash-in-transit vans, all that kind of stuff.

Michael is wearing a balaclava and a tracksuit. He's got his Makarov in his hand, one of the two pistols he acquired for today's robbery. His eyes widen at the sight of Lindsey in the doorway, then at Adrian on the floor.

"What the hell is this?" Michael says. "I thought you were hiding."

Dean sighs. "Things got messy."

"I can see that."

Dean is aware that there are other apartments nearby. Someone might be home, might be listening.

He says, "Come in for a second."

Michael shakes his head. "Do you have any idea how risky it was for me to come here? We need to go."

"Just for a second."

Michael steps over Adrian and goes and stands next to Lindsey.

"Who's she?"

Dean says, "She lives here."

"You let her see your face."

"Doesn't matter," Dean says. "They already know my identity."

"What were you thinking? I mean, Jenna… and, you know…."

Dean's chest twists as if a corkscrew is working its way into him. The fact is, he wasn't thinking. It was pure emotion. He never felt so angry in all his life. And then the gun was going off, and he'd done something terrible. Jenna and…

"It was an accident," Dean whispers.

Michael nods. "I had an accident too. On the way here. Two of them actually."

Dean doesn't like the sound of this. "What happened, Michael?"

"A bit of road rage."

"You got angry at someone?"

"No. Well, yeah. I shouted at a guy, and then he came at me. Another guy was passing, and he saw my face. I couldn't let them get away."

"Christ."

"Yeah."

"They're dead?" Dean asks.

"Oh, yeah."

"Where was that?" Dean asks.

Michael points. "Around the corner."

Dean puts his head in his hands. This was meant to be a simple robbery. Now there's blood on their hands, and they haven't even done the job.

"Where can we go?" Dean hisses.

"We go to the hideout like we planned. The stuff is ready. A change of clothes and all that."

Dean shakes his head. "I'm going to need a new name, a passport..."

"Later," Michael says. "First we get out of here. And we hurry. I don't want to be caught."

Dean freezes at the sound of a chopper approaching. He exchanges a look with Michael.

"They're coming back," Dean says.

He goes over to the kitchen window and looks out. The searchlight sweeps across the area behind the house.

Sirens in the distance.

Getting louder.

So the Gardaí have already caught up with the kid. And they traced him back to where he encountered Dean, because that's the best they can do. Dean expected that to happen, but not so quickly.

Michael's right.

They need to get out of here.

When he turns around, Michael is pointing his gun at Lindsey's head.

Dean says, "What are you doing?"

"We can't leave witnesses."

"It's okay," Dean says. He doesn't want to see Lindsey get hurt. Nor her baby. He's caused enough harm today. "She can't identify you."

"What about you?"

"I told you, they already know my name."

"A hostage could be useful," Michael says thoughtfully. He grabs Lindsey by the arm. Lindsey shows more spunk than Dean would have expected. She struggles to break free from Michael's grasp.

She says, "I'm not going anywhere. I have a baby to look after."

Michael smiles. "Dean, grab the baby."

"What?"

"Take the baby with us. If we get caught, we'll need to negotiate. There's nothing like a dead hostage to show you're serious."

CHAPTER NINETEEN

Lindsey's blood runs cold when she hears Michael's words. She knows the man's name is Michael, because Dean let it slip. Thank god neither of them noticed. If they did, they'd probably kill her.

But Lindsey is not worried about herself. She's worried about her baby. Michael wants to take Jazz with them.

There's nothing like a dead hostage to show you're serious.

Michael adds, "And a live one, to show you're not finished."

Lindsey struggles against Michael, but he holds her tight. His stringy arms are like wires coiled around her waist. Lean and hard as steel.

"Quiet," he hisses in her ear.

All she can do is watch helplessly as Dean goes into the bedroom. He emerges a moment later with Jazz in his arms. He's wrapped her in a blanket. She's awake and gurgling. So sweet and innocent.

Lindsey's heart swells with maternal love, an all-encompassing feeling she couldn't have imagined just weeks ago.

"Leave her alone," Lindsey says.

She hears a helicopter again. The same one? Getting closer, louder. The searchlight hits the kitchen window, flooding the room with light. Then the light is gone again.

"Let her go," Lindsey says. "Let her go."

Dean cradles Jazz in his arms.

Michael holds Lindsey tight.

"Everything is okay," Dean says. "Co-operate and this will be all over very soon."

Lindsey's face burns with anger. "I don't believe you," she says.

"I swear. We'll drop you and your baby off once we get away from here. Now, time to go."

Dean walks past Lindsey, steps over Adrian, and goes out to the hallway. Michael loosens his grip on Lindsey.

"Walk ahead of me and be calm. Don't draw attention to yourself."

Michael looks down at Adrian's still form. He points his gun at Adrian's head.

"Should I?" he calls to Dean.

Dean glances back.

"Don't waste a bullet," he says.

Michael shrugs and tucks the gun into his tracksuit bottoms, then pulls his top down over it. Lindsey walks down the stairs in front of him. She passes a neighbour's door. Then another neighbour's door. Is no one home? What's wrong with them? Surely, they've heard something.

Dean opens the door to the street.

The cold air hits Lindsey when she steps outside. It's a cool March evening, and she wears no jacket, only her jeans and a jumper. She follows Dean down the steps, unable to tear her eyes off the bundle in his arms. She hopes Jazz is warm enough.

If anything happens to her…

No.

It can't.

She won't let it.

She'll do whatever it takes to keep Jazz safe. If she could take a gun from Dean or Michael – what then? Lindsey isn't sure. There's no chance she could shoot a person, but maybe she could threaten them. Force them to let her and Jazz go.

There are three cars parked in the broad driveway. Dean stands uncertainly in front of them until Michael hits his key fob and unlocks a dark Hyundai.

Dean sits in the front passenger seat with Jazz on his lap. Lindsey has no choice but to get in. She can't let Jazz out of her sight. She sits in the back seat and closes the door. The car smells like greasy burgers. Paper crinkles under her feet. The floor is covered in take-away wrappers. Disgusting.

Michael gets behind the wheel, closes the door.

"Let me hold Jazz," Lindsey says.

Dean doesn't even look around.

He says, "Not until we're moving."

The *whoomp whoomp* of helicopter blades is loud. People walking past on the footpath crane their necks to look up at it.

Lindsey's stomach is heaving, exhibiting the family affliction. She can taste carbonara sauce at the back of her throat. So delicious earlier, it now seems foul. She swallows it back down.

"Let's get out of here," Michael says.

He starts the engine and pulls out onto the road. They take the next corner. Lindsey looks down the lane that runs behind her garden. She sees Garda cars, flashing lights, the Emergency Response Unit.

I need you, she thinks. But they can't help her.

The Hyundai leaves them behind, and the lane might as well be a million miles away.

CHAPTER TWENTY

Adrian lies face-down on Lindsey's carpet. He did lose consciousness, he thinks, but only for a second. After that, he was pretending. He waits until the men have left the building before he moves.

The terror that gripped him begins to turn into a bitter kind of resentment. How dare they talk to him like that? How dare they hit him? This is Lindsey's fault. If it wasn't for her, he never would have got into such danger, and nearly been killed by burglars, or whatever the hell those guys are.

Adrian gets to his feet and looks around uncertainly. Lindsey and the men are gone. He knows they took the baby with them. Adrian thinks this could be pretty convenient. If they hurt Lindsey and the baby – which seems like a fair assumption – then Adrian will have no more problems in that regard. Lindsey won't be hounding him for support if she's dead. Adrian's mother will be delighted.

Adrian decides that Lindsey and the kid with the stupid name are as good as dead. Sad but true. He wonders if there's anything here worth taking. It's not like Lindsey's going to need her stuff anymore. Not when she's buried in a hole in the ground with a bullet between her eyes.

He goes through her desk, opening each drawer and looking through it, but finds nothing interesting. It's all study stuff.

He goes into the bedroom.

She has a small bedside unit behind the crib. Three drawers. The first two are full of rubbish like family photos, but in the last one, Adrian finds her banking details, including the PINs to a U.S. bank account and an Irish one. He stuffs the papers in his pocket.

He looks in the wardrobe. All he finds is $80 and €215 in a purse.

Lindsey is such a cheapskate.

He catches sight of himself in the mirror next to her bed.

Blood is running down his face. The sight shocks him. His nose begins to feel sore. Is it broken? What if fragments of bone were driven up into his brain? He needs to get to a doctor.

He hurries out of the apartment.

CHAPTER TWENTY-ONE

The streets shoot past. Outside the speeding car, Lindsey sees people going about their daily lives. Going home after work, shopping, having an evening jog. Everyone looks so normal and happy.

Almost everyone.

She sees a young man wearing a face mask. He's riding a bicycle in the dense traffic. Her gaze lingers on him. Is the mask to protect him from pollution or from the virus? This morning, Lindsey was so worried about the looming pandemic. But in the back seat of Michael's car, she's living a different kind of nightmare.

Michael is driving fast. Dean sits in the front passenger seat, holding a now-crying Jazz to his bloody T-shirt.

"Give her to me," Lindsey says. She leans forward between the seats in front, until her seat belt stops her.

"Don't give her a thing," Michael says.

He brings the car to a stop at a red light. Since they left the house, Michael has been shouting at other drivers, and Jazz has become upset.

Dean's brow wrinkles in thought.

"It doesn't matter," he says to Michael. "They're not going anywhere."

He twists in his seat and hands Jazz to Lindsey.

"Thank you," she says.

"The doors are locked," he reminds her.

Michael gives an exaggerated sigh. "Don't get too attached, Dean. We might have to shoot them."

Lindsey squeezes her eyes shut for a second.

It's okay. It'll be okay. We're okay.

Jazz looks so tiny, so helplessly fragile. Her crying begins to ease as Lindsey rocks her in her arms and murmurs baby-talk to her. She uses her most soothing voice, keeping it low so that it doesn't antagonise the men in the front. Especially Michael. She hates him and she hates the thought that her life, and her daughter's life, depend on the whims of this thug.

The lights change and they start moving again.

"Where are we going?" Lindsey asks. Even after two and a half years here, she's not familiar with Dublin's geography.

"Keep your mouth shut," Michael says. He turns to Dean. "There's a blindfold in the glove compartment. Put it on the girl. I wish we had some rope too, but I wasn't expecting all this."

Dean finds the blindfold. He hands it to Lindsey and tells her, "Put this on."

She covers her eyes. She listens for any clue about where they might be going, straining her ears for anything that might help. All she hears is traffic.

And Michael's words, ringing in her ears.

We might have to shoot them.

CHAPTER TWENTY-TWO

Detective Sergeant Irene Flaherty shines a torch on the corpse on the ground. It's a man, lying on his back in the middle of the road. Stocky build, forties, suit and tie.

He's as dead as it's possible to be. Two entry wounds in the chest, one in the forehead. Any of them would have been fatal. His blood is all over the street.

The guy in the SUV is pretty dead too, though she only sees one entry wound. He's slumped against the side window. Looks like he's taking a nap with his eyes open.

Flaherty was alerted to the scene by uniformed Gardaí checking reports of gunshots. The location of the incident is interesting. It's near where the kid encountered Dean Cullen.

She doesn't think this is a coincidence.

Cullen is still in the area.

She might have caught him by now if they hadn't followed the decoy, but there's nothing she can do about that now. She just needs to make up for the lost time.

A white van approaches. It has *Garda Technical Bureau* written on the side. Forensics. The van comes to a halt a short distance away. The forensics people jump out of the van in their white spacesuits.

Uniformed Gardaí are cordoning off the area as a call comes over Flaherty's radio. It's one of her men, who she has scouting the area.

He says, "I think you better see this."

"Okay," Flaherty replies. Her team doesn't mess around. If they say she needs to see something, then she does.

She walks past the Technical Bureau team, who are busy setting up lights, cameras, and a tent to cover the exposed body.

She gets in her BMW and drives three hundred metres to the address she's been given. It's around the corner. A big old house on a wide Dublin road. One of those buildings with about a dozen steps up to the main door. The door is open and the light is on in the hall.

Flaherty pulls into the driveway and kills the engine.

She brushes a strand of hair out of her eyes, then gets out of the car and makes her way up to the house.

Gary Dwyer is the officer who called her. He's standing in the hallway next to a dog handler with a German Shepherd. Dwyer is a solid officer with three years' experience in the ERU. Flaherty nods at the dog handler who's an older lady Flaherty doesn't know. Flaherty lets the dog sniff her hand.

Next to them is a miserable-looking young man with a bloody nose.

"What's up?" Flaherty asks.

Dwyer gestures to the dog. "Rex here led us to this property, following Dean Cullen's scent from the lane." Dwyer points a finger at the young man. "This is Adrian Connolly. He was just leaving the property when we arrived. Mr. Connolly here had an encounter with two armed men only minutes ago."

"Is that right?" Flaherty asks.

"He overheard one of the men implying that he killed two people."

Flaherty's pulse begins to race. She turns to the man with a new interest.

"Can you tell me what happened?"

The guy stands up a little straighter.

"Yeah," he says. "Those guys attacked me. The guy from the news was one of them. Dean Cullen. And then another guy came along."

"What did the second man look like?"

Adrian shrugs. "I didn't really see him. Just out of the corner of my eye. I think he was thin. He was wearing a balaclava and he was talking to the other guy about whether to kill me."

"Was this before the assault?" Flaherty asks.

Adrian rolls his eyes. "No, after. That guy, Cullen, hit my head against the wall. I mean, I wasn't expecting it or I wouldn't have let it happen."

"Sure," Flaherty says patiently.

"I pretended to be unconscious while they talked. I mean, they had guns. One of those pricks wanted to shoot me, but the other one said not to waste a bullet."

Flaherty looks down the hall. She sees doorways with numbers.

She says, "So they were trying to hide out in your apartment? Can you show me?"

"I can show you," Adrian says, "but it's not my apartment."

She frowns. "Whose apartment is it?"

Another eye roll. Flaherty is starting to wonder how this young man escaped that bullet.

He says, "Lindsey's."

"Lindsey? Who is Lindsey to you?"

"We dated."

"So where's Lindsey now?"

"Oh," he says. "They took her."

"The armed men took Lindsey with them?"

"Yeah, and her baby."

You didn't think to mention that first? Flaherty doesn't say what she's thinking. There's no point turning a supercilious idiot into an uncooperative idiot.

She and Gary Dwyer exchange a look.

Get the rest of the details.

He nods. Good old Dwyer. A solid officer. Three years in the ERU. He knows what she's thinking, sometimes before she does.

"Thank you," Flaherty says. "Garda Dwyer will take a statement. I'll arrange for medics to check you out."

She turns to go. That's when he says, "Michael."

Flaherty swings back around.

"Excuse me?" she says.

"Cullen called the second guy Michael."

"That's very helpful. Did you hear anything else? Did they say where they were going?"

"They were talking about a hideout. Some place where they have a change of clothes. And Cullen said he'd need a passport. They were arguing about that. It was like they already had a place arranged, where they could go after doing some job – like a bank robbery or something. Then things went wrong. But they were going to go to the hideout anyway."

Flaherty nods. "Thank you. That could help us save your girlfriend's life."

Adrian Connolly doesn't react, and Flaherty wonders what's going on there. Why doesn't he look happy at the prospect of his girlfriend surviving?

She stores that thought in the back of her mind for later. Her priority is to find Dean Cullen, the man named Michael, Lindsey and her baby.

Time is running out.

CHAPTER TWENTY-THREE

Lindsey can see nothing. The blindfold is thick, and it blocks out everything. Without sight, the junk-food smell in the car is worse. So is Dean's body odour and Michael's edginess, which comes off him in waves.

She tries to focus on Jazz, a warm bundle in her arms. Lindsey strokes her daughter's back.

Michael's driving is making her nauseous. He speeds along, brakes hard, then accelerates again.

How far have they travelled?

Where are they?

Has it been ten minutes or fifteen?

Impossible for Lindsey to tell. She waits. After a while the car slows, then comes to a stop.

"Alright," Michael says. "Home sweet home."

She hopes that's just an expression, because if she knows where Michael lives, she probably knows too much to live.

A car door opens. Lindsey hears the sound of traffic some distance away. And the sound of Dean exhaling. The door next to Lindsey opens.

"Get out," Michael says.

She reaches up to take off the blindfold, only for Michael to grab her wrist.

"Don't touch that."

"I need to see," Lindsey says.

"You don't need to see anything."

Dean's door opens and closes.

Lindsey reaches out her foot tentatively, feeling for the ground with her toe. With Jazz in her hands, it's awkward. She can feel Michael's presence nearby. Too close. She manages to step out of the car without falling.

The car door slams shut.

Michael moves to her right. He's rustling something, a plastic bag maybe. Dean's light footsteps approach from the left. He presses his hand against the small of Lindsey's back. She allows him to guide her forward.

Michael is a stone-cold killer. He'll take her and Jazz out in a second if it suits him. But Dean isn't so bad, she thinks. Maybe she can arouse some glimmer of a conscience in him.

She takes baby steps, afraid of tripping, dropping Jazz. The ground beneath her is smooth like tarmac.

"Be careful. There's a step a metre ahead," Dean says.

"Okay. Thanks."

Dean moves his hand from her back to her arm, supporting her as she steps cautiously forward. Lindsey hears the jingle of keys. A door unlocking.

"Quick," Michael says. "Get her in."

Dean says to Lindsey, "Turn to your right. Stop. That's it. Now, there's a doorway straight ahead."

Lindsey moves forward.

Her left shoulder bumps against the door jamb. Not hard, because she's moving slowly. Adjusting her course, she steps inside.

She doesn't like being taken to a secret location. It's the kind of thing that happens to a person before they're executed.

"Keep going," Dean says.

His voice doesn't echo, so Lindsey thinks whatever room they are now in must not be very large. He turns her around.

"There's another door," he says.

"Okay."

"Now, there's a chair," Dean says. He guides her down onto it.

Michael is doing something with his plastic bag. Then the rustling stops.

Lindsey waits.

Listens.

And hears a sound like a lid being screwed off a container. The room fills with the smell of petrol.

CHAPTER TWENTY-FOUR

Detective Garda Colm Breen of Donnybrook Garda Station has a voice like a cigar that's been doused in whiskey and driven over by a Harley Davidson. It's Flaherty's second time talking to him today. Breen is familiar with Cullen and his track record. He was instrumental in putting Cullen in jail.

"Breen," is how he answers the phone.

"Detective Sergeant Irene Flaherty here. From ERU. We talked earlier?"

"Yes, we did," Breen says, his voice thick and rich.

Flaherty is behind the wheel of her BMW. It's still in the driveway of Lindsey O'Reilly's building. Since she talked to Adrian Connolly, the so-called boyfriend, she's gathered no more information. The only lead is that the accomplice's name is Michael.

She says, "The Cullen situation has escalated."

"How can I help?"

"Cullen has taken two hostages. A young woman and her baby."

A pause.

Breen says, "I didn't think he had it in him. Of course, given what he did earlier…"

"Right. He's pushing the limits. And now he has an accomplice. A witness overheard a first name: Michael. We don't have much of a description, but this Michael is a male. Thin build. Presumably he's a similar age to Cullen. Does that mean anything to you?"

There's a pause. A terrible pause, during which Flaherty imagines the detective on the other end of the line shaking his head.

She waits.

"Michael Kilpatrick," Breen says at last. "He might be the man you're looking for. He's a scumbag I've always wanted to put away. A nasty piece of work."

"A friend of Cullen?"

"I'm not sure Michael Kilpatrick has any friends, but he and Dean Cullen grew up together. Got in trouble together when they were younger. I suspect they worked on a few jobs before Cullen went to prison."

"That fits. The witness believes they were planning a robbery today. Before things went wrong."

"I still can't believe what he did," Breen says.

"We have two more bodies," Flaherty says.

"Dean Cullen did that?"

"No. Your pal, Michael Kilpatrick. Seems to be a road-rage incident. Two men shot dead. Is that consistent with Kilpatrick?"

"I would say so, though he's never been caught for anything worse than speeding. I couldn't get away with saying this in court but, between you and me, I could see him doing that."

"The thing is, Cullen and Kilpatrick had a hideout ready to go to after the job, and it looks like they're going there now. Would you have any idea where that might be?"

Another long silence.

Come on, Breen.

Tell me what I need to know.

Flaherty decides she'll buy Breen a steak dinner when this is all over, if he can help her.

"I'm sorry," Breen says at last. "I've no idea where the hideout is."

CHAPTER TWENTY-FIVE

Bob's Bets is a typical betting shop. TV screens on one of the side walls, a counter at the end, and a door to a back office. Not an awful lot more than that.

Michael, Dean and Lindsey passed through the shop and now they're in the back office. Lindsey sits on a swivel chair, holding the baby in her arms.

Dean is relieved that Michael's key worked. Michael used to own half this place, but he fell out with his co-owner. That was a few weeks ago and Dean was afraid that the locks might have been changed. But no. One piece of good luck.

Michael upends the black sack and lets their spare clothes fall out on the floor. Immediately, he tears off his tracksuit top and bottoms and stuffs them back in the bag.

"Hurry up," he tells Dean as he tears off his T-shirt.

"We didn't even do the job," Dean says.

"Change clothes anyway. We need to be careful." Michael straightens up and looks at him. "You've got blood on you. I might, too."

Four people are dead.

Dean shakes his head in disgust.

He says, "Michael, I didn't mean to bring you into this. I'm sorry for messing up. I shouldn't have asked you to pick me up."

"Well, you did."

"You shouldn't have come."

"Too right," Michael says.

"Seriously. I'm sorry."

"I wasn't going to leave you hanging," Michael says. He walks over to Dean, wearing only his underwear and socks, and grips Dean by the shoulders. "Listen, we're mates. We've known each other since we were this high."

Michael places his hand at knee height.

"Yeah," Dean says.

Michael says, "We're going to look out for each other, alright? So don't go soft on me now. We're going to get out of this."

Dean nods.

It's nice to hear someone tell him that life will go on.

"Good," Michael says. "Now change your clothes and prepare this area. Let's get this show on the road."

Feeling better, Dean begins to strip.

Michael puts on his clean clothes. He already has the jerrycan of petrol open.

He pats his pockets. "My matches must be in the car," Michael says. "I'll be back in a second."

"Okay."

While Michael goes outside, Dean continues changing. As he does so, he looks at Lindsey, sitting blindfolded, the baby in her arms. Lindsey clears her throat.

"What's the petrol for?" she asks.

"We're going to burn the car."

"What about me? What about my daughter? You said you were going to release us, but you didn't. You brought us here."

"There was no good place to drop you off," Dean lies.

When he has clean clothes on, he picks up the jerrycan of petrol. As quietly as he can, he splashes it on the desks and computers and floor.

Around Lindsey and Jazz.

"What's that?" Lindsey asks, her nostrils flaring.

"Nothing."

"What are you going to do with us?"

Kill them or let them go? Kill them or let them go? The same question has been running through Dean's mind all the way here. He knows Michael's view.

Michael hates witnesses.

"What are you going to do with us?" Lindsey asks again.

Dean swallows.

He doesn't answer.

CHAPTER TWENTY-SIX

Flaherty gets off the phone. She's still in her car, still outside Lindsey's apartment. It's ten minutes since she spoke to Detective Garda Colm Breen.

Uniformed officers have got the registration plate of the car believed to be driven by Michael Kilpatrick. She's established that the car is stolen, so it won't lead back to Kilpatrick directly.

Now she has officers searching for CCTV footage. This is a long, slow job in any large investigation, and it might take months to acquire, catalogue and analyse the relevant footage.

However, she's focusing on the big guns, choosing traffic cameras on each of the main roads leading away from Lindsey's apartment. This might give her an idea of what general direction the car went.

In addition, she has the helicopter continuing its scouting of the area, and she's put out a bulletin for all units to look out for the car Michael Kilpatrick is using – a five-year-old Hyundai, according to witnesses.

At the moment, she's sitting still. The lack of momentum is driving her crazy but there's nowhere to go. All she can do is coordinate her team's efforts.

Flaherty's phone rings for the hundredth time this evening.

She looks at the screen. Colm Breen is calling.

"Flaherty."

"I've been going through the files," Breen says without any greeting. His voice now sounds like a cigar that's been dipped in honey.

"What have you got?" Flaherty says.

Give me something.

"Just a few possibilities. Locations with links to Michael Kilpatrick."

She puts the phone on speaker and gets her notebook and pen ready.

"Go ahead."

First up is a betting shop on the north side of the city. Kilpatrick is part-owner of it. Second is his home address in west Dublin. She got that a few minutes ago from another officer. Third is another betting shop, this one in west Dublin. Kilpatrick was part-owner of this shop too, until a dispute with his fellow owner. Fourth is another betting shop on the south side.

"The scumbag loves gambling," Flaherty says.

She's disappointed with the locations. None of them sound very isolated. She was hoping for something more promising. An abandoned warehouse, a farm in the middle of nowhere –

something like that, where she could imagine hostages being held.

Breen seems to sense her dissatisfaction.

"I know it's not much to go on."

Even when he's apologising, his voice sounds sexy. She has no idea what he looks like, no idea what age he is. But she loves that voice.

"Better than nothing," Flaherty says. "If one of these clues pans out, I owe you a steak dinner. How about it?"

"I'll have to clear that with the wife."

"Oh... Never mind."

"I'm kidding. For the record, I like my steak bloody as hell."

Flaherty laughs. She needs a moment of distraction. "Me too. Got to go."

"Good luck."

Her phone rings again right away. It's a member of the CCTV team. A camera caught Kilpatrick's car heading west. Flaherty reviews the addresses scrawled in her notebook. Two are to the west. Kilpatrick's house and the betting shop.

Breen, you sexy bastard, she thinks.

Now it's Flaherty turn to take a gamble.

CHAPTER TWENTY-SEVEN

Lindsey waits for Dean to answer her question.
What are you going to do with us?
It's a simple question. He shouldn't need to think about it so much. Lindsey's pulse races. Dean said he'll let them go. Why does he seem uncertain now?
Answer me, Lindsey thinks.
When he doesn't, she takes a breath, then reaches up with one hand and pulls off the blindfold.
"Hey," Dean shouts, "don't touch that blindfold or you're dead."
But she has it off before he can get to her. She drops it on the floor and takes in her surroundings.
She's in a small office. The room has a few desks and computers and an ugly navy carpet. There's a door to the front. To the back there's a door and a window with steel bars across it. The door to the back is open, revealing an empty car park.
That must be where Michael is.

Between her and the place where Dean is standing, there's a black sack on the floor with some clothes in it. A jerrycan full of petrol sits next to the bag. With terror, Lindsey sees that it has already been splashed around the office. The computer workstations are soaked in petrol. She feared as much.

"Let us go," Lindsey begs.

"We will," Dean says, but she doesn't like his dull tone of voice.

Make him see you as a person.

Isn't that what hostages are meant to do?

She says, "I guess it's obvious I'm from the States, but could you tell I come from Washington? A little place called Aberdeen. It's quiet there, but it's not so bad. I have two lovely parents. They're right here in Dublin now. They're—"

"Be quiet," Dean says.

But Lindsey forces herself to keep going. "I study history at Trinity. I don't know if I'll get a job here when I'm finished my degree. I hope so, because I really love Dublin."

Dean takes a step closer to her. "I'm warning you."

"I love the people here. They're good people. You're a good person. Please don't kill me. Please don't kill my baby."

"We won't."

"I don't believe you," Lindsey says. "Your friend wants to do it."

Dean rubs his eyes furiously.

Lindsey continues, "I'm only twenty-one. I want to live. Please let me go."

Dean's voice sounds strained. "I said be quiet."
"Do you have a child?" Lindsey says.
Dean blinks quickly.
"I did."

CHAPTER TWENTY-EIGHT

Flaherty's BMW speeds through Dublin's streets. Her team behind her. Lights flashing, sirens screaming. They're heading west, towards the locations Breen put her onto. She still hasn't decided which one to check out first.

Kilpatrick's home address or the betting shop he once had an interest in?

They both lie west of Flaherty's current location, but she'll soon need to choose which one to check first. Flaherty could she split the team in two, but she'd prefer to avoid that. Better to keep everyone together.

She has people checking for CCTV footage. Getting a clue about Kilpatrick's direction was fortunate, but it would be unreasonable to expect any more lucky breaks.

The betting shop is in Harold's Cross, which is closer to Flaherty.

Kilpatrick's house is in Kimmage, two kilometres past the betting shop.

Most sergeants would decide where they were going before they started moving, but not Flaherty. She drives and lets her mind wander. That's how she comes up with her best ideas.

She thinks about Breen and the steak dinner they're going to share. Bloody as hell. It's hard for her to imagine what he looks like, and she tries not to. She doesn't want to be disappointed.

They've nearly reached the turn that leads to Harold's Cross. Flaherty glances in the rear-view mirror. She's driving in front and the team is following. Everyone's waiting for her instructions. She figures his home is the most likely prospect.

She gets on the radio. "We're going to Kilpatrick's house," she says. "Repeat, location is Kilpatrick's house."

They drive past the turn to the betting shop.

CHAPTER TWENTY-NINE

Dean did have a child, a two-and-a-half-year-old son named Jonathan. Jenna brought little Jonathan to the prison every week. She was good like that. The boy was the reason Dean was able to get through his prison sentence, and he was the reason Dean went to Jenna's place today.

He had been released three days ago. Six months early, thanks to the virus. The prison authorities wanted to clear the deck as best they could. Dean's sentence was for nothing worse than burglary, so he was lucky to be chosen for an early release.

He tried to get in touch with Jenna as soon as he left the jail. He didn't expect to move in with her again, not straight away. She'd made that clear during her visits. But he was surprised she didn't answer her phone. He decided to pay a visit to Jenna's bungalow in Portobello.

It's a tidy little house with a side gate. Dean went there today, on his way to Ballsbridge, where the job with Michael was meant to take place. He had the Makarov tucked into his jeans and hidden by his jacket.

Dean heard Jonathan's laughter from the back garden when he arrived. What a sweet sound.

He was about to ring the doorbell, but he came up with a better idea. Jonathan and Jenna would be so surprised if he appeared unannounced.

He went around the side gate and jumped over it. Then he walked down the side of the house. It was a lovely March afternoon and the sight of the garden reminded Dean of the happy times he'd had here.

When the weather was pleasant, he and Jenna left the sliding doors in the bedroom open. They led right out into the garden.

Those doors were open now.

The garden looked different to the last time he'd seen it. There were more flowers in it and unfamiliar toys lay scattered across the lawn.

Dean walked over to the open doorway. A man was inside the bedroom. He was about Dean's age, with tattoos down his arms. He was naked.

Blood swam to Dean's head.

A raging, primal thirst for violence.

The naked man was lounging on the bed Dean and Jenna had chosen together years ago. He was smiling and his hair was damp, as if he had just had a shower. He looked up and saw Dean. His eyes widening, he scrambled off the bed, calling Jenna's name.

Dean pulled the Makarov from the waistband of his jeans and stepped into the room.

The man was scrambling to escape, making an almost comical attempt to put on his trousers.

Dean stepped closer still, raised the Makarov and fired four shots in rapid succession.

It felt like it happened in slow motion, as the man dived out of the bullets' way. At the same time, Jenna came into the bedroom from the hall, carrying Jonathan in her arms. She had a confused expression on her face.

"Dean?" she said, as the first bullet hit Jonathan's abdomen. The second went into his mouth. Jenna's body was turning, and the third and fourth shots pierced her side.

She coughed a fine spray of blood, before hitting the floor. Dean stepped closer. For a few seconds, there was still life in Jenna's eyes.

Then it blinked out.

Dean was vaguely aware that the man was running away.

He stared at Jenna and Jonathan on the bedroom floor. Eyes open. Confusion on Jenna's face. A blank expression on Jonathan's.

They were dead.

Dean has a confused recollection of running from the house, of driving madly towards Ballsbridge. He doesn't know why he did that. Maybe he thought Michael could help somehow. Of course, no one could help.

By the time he reached Ballsbridge, the Gardaí were already after him. He discovered that when patrol car pulled him over. Two uniformed Gardaí had got out of the car. One was calling it in over the radio. The other approached Dean.

Dean hit the accelerator.

It was a great getaway, except he crashed his car two hundred metres down the road. Wrapped it around a lamppost.

Then he was on foot.

Running, running, running.

He saw a lane.

CHAPTER THIRTY

Dean seems lost in thought. When he said he had a kid, his face clouded over. Lindsey doesn't like the way he used the past tense. *Had.* She's afraid to ask what that means, but she can guess. Something terrible happened. That must be what brought him to this.

If anything happened to Jazz, Lindsey would lose it too. She has to make sure that doesn't happen. Michael is still outside. She's sure he'll be back soon. If she does nothing, she's dead and so is Jazz.

"I'm going to get up now," Lindsey says.

Dean's eyes focus on her. He says, "Don't even think about it."

She's afraid of the bullets, afraid of the petrol fumes, afraid of the fire she's sure will come. She rises to her feet, holding Jazz with both hands.

"Dean, I don't think you really want to hurt me. I'm sorry for whatever happened to you. I don't know what to say about that. But I'm not going to wait here to die."

Dean is pointing his pistol at her head, but his face is sweaty and uncertain. He wipes his face with the back of his free hand.

"I'm going to go," Lindsey says.

"Don't." Dean shakes his head. "Wait for Michael."

"Say again? You want me to wait for Michael to kill me?"

She turns and takes a step towards the open doorway. She squeezes her eyes shut, bracing herself for Dean's shot.

The door isn't far away.

Ten paces maybe.

One, two, three slow steps.

Lindsey allows herself to think that maybe it will be okay. Dean won't hurt her. She'll walk out of here alive.

Four, five, six.

It's working. She's getting there. She holds Jazz tighter.

Seven, eight, nine—

A dark shape appears in the doorway.

Michael.

"Where do you think you're going?" he shouts.

She backs away, towards Dean. Michael is shaking his head. He gives Dean a look of absolute disgust.

"If you weren't a mate…" he says, shaking his head.

Michael stands between Lindsey and the door. He holds a matchbox in his hands. As she watches, he takes out a single match.

Lindsey backs away farther, moving past the window. She can't get out through the window. Not with those steel bars on it. She's backed into the corner of the room.

The situation is hopeless.

There's no way out.

Michael lights the match.

"I was going to shoot you first," he says. "But now I think I'll burn you alive."

CHAPTER THIRTY-ONE

The night sky seems darker than it should be. Darker than black. Flaherty is crouched behind her BMW at the side of a dimly lit car park. Bob's Bets is one in a row of small businesses in front of her.

Flaherty is here because a silent alarm was triggered in the betting shop. The alarm company contacted the Gardaí and the connection with Michael Kilpatrick meant that Flaherty got a call. She turned the car away from Kilpatrick's house and headed towards the betting shop at once.

It made sense that Kilpatrick came here. He'd had a falling out with his former business partner who owned half of this betting shop. Maybe Kilpatrick was taking the opportunity to settle a score while using the place as a hideout. Maybe steal some cash, trash the place – who knew?

It was a more attractive prospect than Kilpatrick taking hostages and a stolen car to his home, even temporarily.

So here Flaherty is. She hopes she's not too late.

The car park wraps around the front and back of the building. It's empty now except for the stolen Hyundai and another vehicle – no doubt Kilpatrick's escape vehicle.

Flaherty's people surround the building. Front and back. Flaherty is at the back, with most of the team. They're all keeping their distance. They couldn't get too close, or Michael Kilpatrick would have seen them, but now he's gone inside.

His head is visible through the window.

She presses the walkie-talkie to her ear.

"Fire when ready," she says.

She's talking to Gary Dwyer, the officer who spoke to Adrian Donnelly earlier. Dwyer's bolt-action rifle is aimed at the window.

She waits and watches, her body tense.

He takes the shot.

There's the crack of the shock wave as the bullet pierces the window, leaving a neat hole in it. Through binoculars, Flaherty sees Michael Kilpatrick fall to the ground. She has no doubt that he has a neat hole in him too.

Dwyer is good like that.

"Go, go, go," she shouts over the radio. "Extreme caution. We have two vulnerable hostages."

She watches members of the Emergency Response Unit run across the car park. Dark shadows against a dark background.

Flaherty runs forward too, braced for the worst.

CHAPTER THIRTY-TWO

Lindsey shrinks back against the wall, clutching Jazz to her chest, as Michael collapses the floor. There's a hole in the window and a hole in Michael's head. His blood is on Lindsey's face and in her mouth.

Worse, Michael got the match lit before he was shot. It falls from between his fingers and lands in a puddle of petrol, which ignites with an enthusiastic *whoosh*.

Flames erupt and blaze across the room, blocking Lindsey's path to the door. She has to skirt around the flames.

Dean is staring at Michael's body in disbelief.

Lindsey has no choice but to pass him. She runs towards him, flames on her left side, the wall of the room on her right.

He sees her coming and raises the gun. With her free hand, Lindsey picks up the black sack of clothes. The contents of the bag are on fire, and she burns her hand lifting it. Ignoring the pain, she lobs the sack at Dean.

His hands go up, and he fires off a shot into the ceiling.

Lindsey hurries past, Jazz like a football in her arms.

A wooden computer desk collapses in her path. The air is full of black smoke that snakes into Lindsey's lungs and makes her cough. She drops to her knees and begins to crawl towards the door, her eyes burning, trying not to touch anything hot. She scrambles over the collapsed desk.

Shouts come from the car park.

Someone with a megaphone.

Help?

Lindsey can hardly believe it.

She moves towards the sound. Towards freedom. She's so close.

Then a hand grabs her ankle.

Pulls her back.

She drops Jazz on the carpet. Lindsey is terrified Jazz is hurt. The baby continues crying, though, and Lindsey hopes that's a good sign.

She turns on her side.

Dean is also on his hands and knees, trying to escape the smoke.

"Let go of me," Lindsey shouts over the roar of the flames.

"I'm sorry," he says. "I need a hostage."

She kicks out with one foot. Misses Dean's face but hits his hand, making him drop the gun. He reaches for it, but she kicks out again and this time she does get him in the face. He topples back, stunned.

While he's recovering, she reaches over and grabs the gun. She points it at him.

"Give it to me," Dean says. "You'll only hurt yourself."

Lindsey has never held a gun. She doesn't know what she's doing. She only knows she needs to protect her daughter, needs to protect herself.

"Don't make me do it," she shouts. By this time she can barely breathe, can barely see. The smoke fills the air. Everything is a blur.

Dean makes a grab for her.

She closes her eyes and squeezes the trigger. She opens her eyes to find that the bullet has gone harmlessly past him.

Dean pins down her legs, crawls up over her and slaps her across the face.

The blow dazes her.

Lindsey doesn't let go of the gun, though. She can't. She feels like closing her eyes, feels so tired, but she fights the feeling. Everything depends on this moment.

As Dean straddles her, she raises the gun. This time, she keeps her eyes open. She aims for Dean's heart.

Lindsey squeezes the trigger and the bullet hits him, knocks him backwards, into the flames. He doesn't move again.

She drops the gun and turns to find Jazz being stolen away by a dark figure.

"No!" Lindsey screams.

Another figure emerges out of the smoke. A woman dressed in black.

She grabs hold of Lindsey and lifts her to her feet.

"It's okay," the woman shouts. "You're safe."

The lack of oxygen overwhelms Lindsey and she passes out.

When she comes to, it's only seconds later. She's lying on her back, with the stars overhead. A paramedic slips an oxygen mask over her mouth and nose. Jazz is next to her, in the arms of a second paramedic.

Lindsey turns her head to the side.

There are armed Gardaí and the fire brigade.

So many lights, she thinks, before losing consciousness again.

CHAPTER THIRTY-THREE

A week later, Lindsey O'Reilly sits in the passenger seat of a dark BMW 3 Series. The interior smells like apple air freshener. Detective Sergeant Irene Flaherty is behind the wheel. Late afternoon, and the car is parked outside a house in Ballsbridge.

Lindsey is wearing a surgical face mask as a precaution against the spread of the coronavirus. It's the second week of March and it's impossible to find hand sanitiser in the shops. Everyone seems to be stocking up on toilet paper and flour, and obsessively watching the ever-changing advice of experts.

Lindsey is less worried about Covid-19 than she was a week earlier. She's doing her best, and that's all she can do. She's decided not to worry about things she cannot change.

Flaherty doesn't wear a mask, but she has a scarf pulled up around her mouth and nose. Sitting in the car, the windows are rolled down and both women are covering their mouths and noses.

Lindsey finds the detective excellent company. Of course, she'd find anyone who saved her life and her baby's life excellent company.

Jazz is at home now, being watched by her grandparents. They were surprised when Lindsey said she was going to stay in Dublin. They expected the experience to make her want to leave. But she has decided that nothing is going to force her out of her home again. She's going to be more assertive about doing what she wants to do from now on. Right now, she wants to be here.

"Here we go," Flaherty says.

A patrol car drives up the road and pulls into the driveway of the house they're watching.

Two uniformed officers get out, walk up to the door and ring a bell. When it opens, Adrian Connolly stands there. The expression on his face is priceless. It's what Lindsey is here to see.

Lindsey's bank accounts were emptied over the last week. Cash she had in her apartment has also gone missing, and she can't blame Dean Cullen for it. Thankfully her parents have been able to keep her afloat.

And the investigation is moving along nicely.

She watches as the two officers handcuff Adrian and escort him to their car. They help him into the back seat, then get in the car and drive away.

Lindsey turns to Flaherty. "Thank you," she says. "That was so good to see."

"Thought it would make you feel all warm inside. I'll drive you home."

As Flaherty knows, it's a short drive. They don't talk on the way. In a minute, they reach Lindsey's building.

"Take care of yourself," Flaherty says.

Lindsey steps out of the car.

"Would you like to come in for a coffee?" she asks.

Flaherty smiles. "I can't. I have to buy someone a steak dinner. But thanks."

They wave their goodbyes and Lindsey heads up the steps of her building. She takes off her face mask outside the door to her apartment.

She opens the door to find Mom throwing Jazz in the air and catching her as she falls. Dad stands next to them, laughing his head off. Jazz looks so happy too, laughing and cooing as she bounces up and down.

Lindsey watches them for a moment, a smile spreading across her face. Then she steps forward, towards her family, into the future.

THE END

HIT AND RUN

CHAPTER ONE

I'm dying, Jake Whelan thought.

He had only climbed one flight of stairs, but his suit felt tight and his lungs screamed for air. Maybe this was how a heart attack felt.

He pushed himself to continue, up one more flight of stairs.

On the fifth floor, Jake stopped and leaned against the wall. He still felt like he was dying, but it was probably all in his head. Climbing a couple of dozen steps shouldn't kill a healthy thirty-two-year-old. He was a healthy weight and suffered from no underlying health condition.

The smell in the stairwell was unpleasant – like new carpet – but Jake was glad he hadn't taken the elevator. Confined spaces were murder these days.

He pushed open the door and set off down the fifth-floor corridor.

"Hey, handsome."

Liz Dubois was coming from the bank of elevators. His girlfriend of a year wore a long golden skirt and a green blouse which complemented her flowing brown hair. She adjusted her glasses, and said, "You weren't in your office. I thought I'd catch you here."

Jake took a breath.

"You scared the hell out of me," he said.

Liz frowned. "I don't know why you're so jumpy."

He took the envelope she held out to him. A *Good Luck* card was inside. In careful, curly letters, Liz had written, *To Jake, my partner.* She'd doodled a cartoon heart next to her signature.

Jake forced a smile. "Thanks, Liz."

She threw her arms around him, squeezing him so tight that it hurt.

"I just wanted to wish you luck. I know you don't need it. I'm sure you'll get the promotion."

As always, Liz's words were clipped and precise, her accent the product of a French father and a German mother.

"How's your dad?" Jake asked, pulling away from her.

"His aide says he's in good spirits."

Wednesday nights, Liz had her weekly teleconference with her father. Christian Dubois had lived in the Grüne Felder private hospital in Munich for years, battling ALS. He was almost completely paralysed and could only communicate now by blinking. Fortunately, his aide was a French-speaker, who was able to interpret Mr. Dubois's eye movements. He meticulously transcribed messages so Liz and her father could communicate during the weekly call.

"I'm glad," Jake said. "Well, I better go in."

"I'll wait with you."

"You might be missed in reception," Jake told her.

"It's been dead quiet all day," Liz said.

"You never know when you might be needed."

"I guess you're right. I'll see you later? We can celebrate."

"Sure," Jake said, feeling a stab of disappointment. He'd enjoyed having a couple of hours to himself the previous evening.

Jake watched Liz walk back to the elevator. She hit the button for the lobby and blew Jake a kiss while she waited.

Liz worked behind the reception desk on the ground floor. Jake had been seeing her for a year and had wanted to end things for almost that long. However, the situation with her father made Jake reluctant to break things off. She was a good daughter, saving every cent she made to pay his medical expenses. From the way Liz talked, Jake understood that Mr. Dubois was extremely close to the end of his life.

Once Liz was gone, Jake stepped into the conference room. The empty room lay in darkness. Through the floor-to-ceiling window, Jake saw the lights of Dublin city. They were reflected in the table that ran the length of the room.

He winced at the stale air.

The whole building was stuffy, but this room was especially bad. Sterile, like something Nasa would make if they were trying to simulate the moon. He just couldn't seem to breathe.

Jake flicked on the light. While the fluorescent bulbs flickered to life, he made his way to the other end of the room and opened a window. It only budged a centimetre, to ensure that no one could jump to their death. Grennan and Brennan might have lost some employees over the years otherwise.

Jake smiled at the thought, but it wasn't funny. He'd felt like doing that himself a few times.

The basin of the Grand Canal was below him, a short distance from where the canal met the river. Its water looked calm. The area was quiet today, even the office towers housing the big tech companies. Understandable, the second day after Christmas.

Loosening his tie, Jake leaned forward so his face was near the open window. He tried to suck the freezing air deep into his lungs, but his breathing remained shallow. These last months, he'd felt like he might drop dead any second. His heart was constantly pounding like a rabbit's, his lungs struggling to supply him with oxygen.

Jake's life was enviable. A job at a prestigious law firm. A comfortable apartment. An attentive girlfriend. But somehow this wasn't how he expected life to be.

He walked over to the head of the table and sat in Arthur Grennan's seat. The only comfortable chair in the room, padded with red leather and soft filling.

Jake ran a finger over the polished mahogany tabletop. He couldn't wait to be sitting in this chair for real.

In school, he'd told his guidance counsellor he wanted to work outdoors, doing something on the land. Be a farmer, a park ranger. Stupid idea, but that was where he was happiest. Hiking in the hills, camping by the sea. He kept a Swiss Army knife in the drawer of his desk, as a reminder.

A dark figure in the doorway startled Jake out of his day dream. It was his colleague, Charlotte Flynn.

She said, "Arthur wouldn't like to find you in his chair."

Jake shrugged. "Just seeing how it feels."

Charlotte looked like she'd stepped out of a magazine cover. Her long, brown hair hung in glossy curls on the shoulders of her tailored suit. She wore a crisp navy blouse underneath and a necklace worth more than Jake's apartment.

A stunner, no doubt about it. He'd been attracted to Charlotte since she joined the firm in March. Jake had been dating Liz then. Already trying to get out of it, but it was around then that her father began to really deteriorate.

Charlotte might also have been the best-connected person Jake knew. Her mother was the Chief Justice of Ireland, her father a prominent senator.

No wonder then, that Charlotte walked into the room like she owned the place. She lowered herself into the seat at Jake's side and crossed her legs.

"Better close the window," Charlotte said.

"I need fresh air."

"Arthur gets a chill easily."

"I don't care," Jake snapped.

Charlotte smiled. "You're going to be disappointed today."

"I don't think so."

"Want to bet on it?"

"Sure," Jake said. "How does ten euro sound?"

"Fine for schoolboys. How about ten thousand?"

It took a moment for Jake to realise she wasn't joking. He sat up straighter in his chair. "For real? Ten grand?"

Charlotte cocked an eyebrow. She was for real alright. Jake had about three hundred euro in his bank account. Not that he didn't earn a generous salary, but he couldn't seem to hold onto it. Anyway, it didn't matter whether he had the money. He was certain he'd win the bet. Charlotte was an excellent solicitor, smart and diligent, but she was a newcomer. Jake had been at the firm for a decade, and the promotion was his.

"Fine," Jake said at last.

Charlotte held out a pale hand. Jake reached across the table, took it in his. Her skin was dry, her grip firm.

"Congratulations," Charlotte said. "You just lost ten thousand euro."

Bravado. That was all it was. Charlotte was overconfident.

Jake got to his feet and pushed Grennan's chair in. He walked around to the other side of the table from Charlotte and took a seat as their colleagues began to arrive. Jake greeted people as they entered the room. Charlotte ignored everyone and played with her phone.

The murmuring built as more people arrived. At last, Arthur Grennan walked into the room. The door slammed shut behind him and everyone stopped talking. Grennan was sixty-two years old, thin and slightly stooped, with wisps of white hair doing nothing to hide his scalp. But he showed no sign of stepping down and he still had enough energy to stuff himself into a three-piece suit every day.

Grennan walked up to the top of the table, stopped and looked around, his face puckered up like he'd just bitten into a lemon.

"Christ, there's a draft in here."

"Let me get that," Jake said.

Forcing a smile, he hurried over to the window and closed it. As he sat back down, he sensed Charlotte's eyes on him. He avoided her mocking gaze.

"Now," Grennan said, as he reached the top of the table. "Let us get straight to the point. We are here to welcome the newest partner to this firm."

"Here, here!" someone said.

Jake took a deep breath.

He prepared to stand up.

Arthur Grennan said, "Please join me in congratulating Charlotte Flynn."

CHAPTER TWO

Liz Dubois hadn't been able to resist coming back up to the fifth floor. There was nothing happening downstairs. No reason for her to waste her time in reception. Everyone else was gathered in the conference room.

She lurked in the corridor until everyone was inside, then pressed her ear against the door. She could hardly wait to hear Jake being made a partner. They could celebrate all night. Maybe Jake would stay at her place. She'd missed him the previous evening, but Wednesday nights belonged to her father, and there was nothing she could do about that.

Arthur Grennan began speaking.

Liz held her breath and pressed the side of her head tight against the door.

She gaped in shock when he said Charlotte's name.

How had this happened? Liz couldn't believe Charlotte had stolen the promotion from Jake. It must have been because of her clout. With wealthy, influential parents like hers, Charlotte had never needed to work hard at anything.

It wasn't fair.

Liz strode away from the door, a cold rage sweeping over her as she got into the elevator. She hit the button for the third floor, where the mergers and acquisitions solicitors were based. She wanted to teach Charlotte a lesson.

On the third floor, Liz made her way past the deserted desks to Charlotte's office. It was a sterile room, containing no sign of life. A steel desk, a swivel chair, some shelves and a filing cabinet. No plants. No photos of loved ones. Charlotte had fancy degrees on the wall, and awards lining her shelves.

Liz stood in front of Charlotte's desk.

The computer was on and Liz felt so furious, she thought she might put her fist through the monitor.

Then she caught sight of Charlotte's coat hanging on the rack. Long, belted and black. The label said it was Givenchy. It must have cost Charlotte a fortune. Thousands of euro. It would be a shame if something happened to it.

Liz looked around on the desk for a pair of scissors but couldn't find any. She walked down the hall to Jake's office.

His Swiss Army knife was in its usual place in his top drawer.

CHAPTER THREE

Charlotte pushed back her chair and stood up as her colleagues broke out in applause. They put on a decent show, looking like they were pleased for her – when, really, they all wanted to be where she was.

When Arthur said Charlotte's name, Jake jumped to his feet with a smile. It took a moment for him to realise his name hadn't been called.

"You can sit down," Charlotte said.

Jake did – while everyone laughed.

A little cruel, but Charlotte couldn't afford to show weakness in a room like this.

She shook hands with Arthur. This was a great moment, even if Grennan and Brennan was only the second most prestigious law firm in the country.

"Congratulations, Charlotte."

"Thanks, Arthur."

Up close, his eyes were red and watery, his scalp dotted with liver spots. Two waiters appeared at the back of the room, wheeling in a trolley with ice buckets and champagne flutes. They brought it to the side of the room. Corks shot into the air. Glasses were filled. Everyone got to their feet.

Arthur accepted the first glass of champagne, Charlotte the second.

"I'm driving," she said.

"So is everyone." Arthur smiled. "But a little won't hurt. It's a tradition."

Charlotte had no choice. If these people saw her refuse a glass of champagne, they'd assume she was an alcoholic. Rumours would spread, clients would get edgy. She'd be finished.

"I wouldn't want to stand in the way of tradition," Charlotte said, flashing him her best smile.

Arthur raised his glass to make the toast. "Everyone, please join me in congratulating Charlotte. Not just our new partner, Charlotte will be heading up the Mergers and Acquisitions Department."

With applause ringing in her ears and a smile frozen on her face, Charlotte watched Jake slip out the door.

An uneasy feeling spread across her chest. Surely, he'd known he was never going to be made partner. Charlotte was the logical choice, the most capable solicitor and the one with the best connections. Arthur would have been a fool not to make her partner.

Still, Charlotte took no pleasure in causing Jake distress. She would have already moved on from this firm if he wasn't here.

She took a sip from her glass. The drink fizzed and bubbled in her mouth, the alcohol flavour barely tolerable. Arthur leaned closer to her.

"We're going to be doing some pruning around here," he said in a low voice.

Charlotte nodded slowly. "What did you have in mind?"

"Get rid of the dead wood," Arthur said. "Start with Whelan. He's not pulling his weight."

"You want me to fire Jake?"

"You don't have to do it tonight. But some time before the end of the year."

About as generous as ever.

"Does he really need to go?" Charlotte asked. "You know how bad layoffs can look."

Arthur shrugged. "If you can find a better way to boost the bottom line, it's up to you."

"Understood," Charlotte replied.

As soon as Arthur left to talk to someone else, Charlotte got stuck in a conversation with another senior partner, then a few associates who gathered around her. Charlotte could smell their desperation, their desire for her success to rub off on them.

As soon as she could, Charlotte slipped away to check on Jake. She took the elevator down to the third floor. Jake's office was the same as hers, a grey box with sleek grey furniture, a grey carpet and lots of glass and steel. Jake wasn't at his desk. His jacket was gone.

The Swiss Army knife he was always playing with sat on his desk.

Charlotte made her way to her own office. She saw at once that her new coat hung in tatters.

Someone had cut it up good, stabbing and slicing it mercilessly. Its gold buttons lay all over floor.

Jake.

A feeling of rage swelled within Charlotte's chest. Her mother had taught her never to let a slight go unchecked.

I'll kill that bastard, she thought.

CHAPTER FOUR

Jake stepped out of the elevator on the ground floor. He ignored Liz, who was calling his name, and hurried past the reception desk, out into the night.

The temperature had been hovering around freezing all week, and though there had been no snow on Christmas Day, there was plenty of frost. Jake walked quickly across the pedestrian plaza, next to the canal basin, being cautious not to slip on the ice.

Ten thousand euro, Jake thought. *I've lost ten thousand euro. And didn't get the job I've been working towards for a decade.*

His breathing became more laboured. He pulled out his phone and called Dr. Katherine O'Brien. The counsellor made him call her Kathy. Her clinic would be closed until early January, but Jake couldn't wait that long.

Phone pressed to his ear, he headed for the main road, which ran alongside the pedestrian area. Finally, Kathy picked up.

"I'm sorry to interrupt your holidays," Jake said. "But this is an emergency."

"Slow down. What's happening?"

When Kathy heard the state he was in, she agreed to meet him at a nearby café.

With his hands plunged deep into his pockets, Jake hurried past the tall office blocks. Many big multinationals had extensive office space in the area. Jake wasn't complaining, as they all needed legal advice. But Jake would have preferred to be far away, trekking in the mountains, the smell of pine cones in the air and the soft forest floor under his boots.

These days, he never had time for that. He spent evenings and weekends reading legal documents, in what little time he could steal away from Liz.

As Jake approached the café, he saw Kathy sitting at a stool by the window. He waved and ducked inside.

Aside from a student tapping away on his laptop, they were the only customers.

Jake felt a little better as soon as he caught sight of Kathy. In her mid-forties, she had twinkling amber eyes and an easy smile, her kind face framed by curly red hair. Today she was bundled up in a padded coat. A hat and gloves rested next to a Manilla folder and a steaming cup of tea.

"I planned to treat you," Jake said.

"Never mind. I couldn't wait."

"What are you drinking?"

"Chamomile. You might like to try it sometime."

"I will," Jake said.

But when he went to the counter, he ordered an Americano out of habit.

"This is not what I do," Kathy said, when Jake took the stool next to her. "I'm not an emergency support service."

"I get that," Jake said. "I'm sorry."

"Having said that, I'm willing to make an exception this one time. I've pencilled in twenty minutes and I'm afraid that's all the time I can give you. My kids will be home soon."

"Of course."

"Tell me why you asked to see me."

Kathy listened while Jake spoke about getting passed over for promotion. "It's not just the promotion. It's... I don't know. It's like a cloud hanging over me."

"Like you've told me before?"

"Yeah, but worse. I feel like I'm physically dying now."

"I think being passed over for promotion is a trigger, like some of the other triggers we've discussed."

"It's worse than I've ever felt before. That's what scared me."

He told her how he had feared he'd collapse in the stairwell. Kathy listened and jotted down notes on her pad.

"Remember the progress we've made over the last few weeks," Kathy said. "And remember the tools and techniques that you've successfully employed. The breathing techniques, the meditation, the mindfulness. So whatever the trigger is, we approach the same way, by first observing it and then reviewing our response."

Jake nodded, already feeling better. Amazing how much good a little talking could do. He had no family and he couldn't imagine burdening his friends with this stuff.

When time was up, Jake and Kathy muffled up against the cold and walked outside.

"I'll walk you to your bike," Jake said.

He followed her around the corner, to where a bicycle was chained to a lamppost. The district was eerily quiet.

"That's me," Kathy said.

Jake waited while she removed the lock and got on the saddle. He was glad he'd reached out to her. She had even refused payment for the session.

"Okay," she said, stuffing her notebook in her jacket pocket. "Take care, and make sure to take some time for yourself. This is very important. Self care. I know you hate buzzwords but take some Jake-time."

He smiled. "I will. Thank you."

"Next week, call and make an appointment," she told him.

Kathy cycled out onto the road. As she pedalled, her notebook fell out of her pocket.

"Hey," Jake called.

Kathy glanced over her shoulder. The bike wobbled.

Jake said, "You dropped—"

Then he heard the roar of an engine. A white car tore down the road from the direction of his office.

"Watch out!" Jake shouted.

Kathy raised her arm to shield her eyes from the glare of the headlights, as the car smashed into her.

CHAPTER FIVE

Jake squeezed his eyes shut at the moment of the impact. He heard the dull thump of the car hitting Kathy's body, the chime of her bicycle bell, then the screech of brakes as the car came to a halt.

Kathy was lying motionless on the road when Jake opened his eyes. He stared in horror. The car that had hit her was a white Honda Civic. Jake stepped closer, saw that registration plate indicating that it was seven years old, saw the worn tires and the scratch on the back-right door.

Jake knew this car.

The driver's door opened, and Liz stepped out.

"Oh my god," she gasped.

"Liz?"

Jake's voice was raw. His head felt like it had just finished a spin-and-drain cycle in a washing machine.

He sprinted to the place where Kathy lay motionless. Liz was right behind him. She hunkered down and checked Kathy's pulse. Liz's face was grim when she met Jake's eyes.

"She's dead."

"No." Jake pulled out his phone.

Liz said, "What are you doing?"

"Calling an ambulance. What do you think?"

"No," she said. "We can't help her. She's dead, Jake. Dead. I'm sorry. But no one's going to resuscitate her. Her spine's broken."

Jake supposed he was in shock, as he couldn't seem to think straight. "What are you even doing here?"

"I followed you, of course. You ran off without waiting for me."

"We need to call this in."

"We can't," Liz said. "We'll be in trouble."

"You mean you'll be in trouble."

Liz gave him a hard look. "You distracted me. I saw you at the side of the road, waving your arms in the air." Liz gripped Jake's wrist. "I'm sorry. I'm not blaming you. But the woman's dead. We can't help her. It doesn't make any difference if we tell anyone. All that will happen is we'll get arrested. I can't afford that."

Jake rubbed his eyes, wishing this was just a bad dream. He said, "What do you mean?"

"My dad, Jake. You know his situation. He's able to have an aide looking after him because of my salary. The aide is the only one who can read his eye movements, the only one in the hospital who speaks French. If I'm not sending money, then my dad—"

Jake let out an animal howl of frustration.

He said, "We can't just leave Kathy like this."

Liz touched him on the arm. "I'm sorry. But we have to."

"I'll call it in. Anonymously."

"They'll trace your phone."

"Then drive me to a fucking payphone, Liz."

"Alright, alright," she said. "Don't shout at me."

Jake staggered to front passenger seat of the Honda Civic. Liz got behind the wheel and reversed to the junction behind them.

"Hurry," he said. "Find a phone."

"There are hardly any public phones in Dublin anymore."

"There's one down the road, I think."

"They might still be able to identify you," she said. "What if there's CCTV covering the phone?"

"I don't care. I'm not leaving Kathy there."

"Who is she? What were you doing with her?"

"She's my therapist." Jake's voice caught. "Or she was."

"What?"

Liz turned in surprise.

"God, Liz. Keep your eyes on the road."

"You just never told me you were seeing a therapist. How long were you seeing her? What was it for?"

"It doesn't matter," Jake snapped. He spotted a payphone. "There."

He jumped out of the car before it even stopped moving. He rang for an ambulance, and when the dispatcher started asking questions, he hung up.

Once he was back in the passenger seat, Liz sped away from the area. Jake didn't know where to go, what to do. Part of him wanted to go back to the place where Kathy's body lay, so he could stay with her until an ambulance arrived. He couldn't believe she was dead.

If she hadn't tried to help him, she'd be fine. She'd be with her kids, enjoying the holidays.

"It was a terrible accident," Liz said. "We can't tell anyone about this."

Jake didn't reply.

He hated her for following him. And he hated her for making him leave the scene of the accident. The anger stewed inside him as Liz drove aimlessly around.

Perhaps she was right. What was the point of hanging around when it made no difference to Kathy? He didn't want to see Liz go to jail.

Emerging from a daze, Jake realised they were approaching his apartment. A big old Georgian house on the edge of the city centre, where Jake rented a small apartment.

Liz parked on the street.

In silence, Jake trudged up to his apartment, Liz following close behind.

He opened the door and let her in first. She sat on the couch, curling her feet under her. Jake joined her. For a while, neither of them spoke. The radio in the kitchen was on. Jake sometimes left it on all day as it made the apartment feel less empty when he arrived home with his microwave dinner-for-one.

"Are you okay?" Liz said.

Jake sighed. Said nothing.

The news came on and Jake heard the words "hit and run".

"Did you hear that?" Jake asked. Reporters had already caught wind of the accident. It must have been a slow news day.

"What?"

"Shush." He strained to hear the reporter's words.

"... the woman has been taken to St. Vincent's Hospital and is understood to be in a critical condition. And now for the weather..."

"Oh my god," Jake said.

Kathy was alive.

CHAPTER SIX

When Charlotte saw her ruined coat, she flew into her worst rage for quite a while. She took hold of her swivel chair and slammed it against her desk. Her computer monitor wobbled and her Lawyer of the Year trophy fell to the floor.

Charlotte had planned to do some work, but she was furious at Jake, and she decided she wasn't going to let it go. She rolled up her coat and walked out the door, carrying it under her arm. She took the stairs down to the underground car park. Her silver Jaguar XJ gleamed under a ceiling light.

She threw her coat on the backseat and took a moment to collect herself.

The car smelled faintly of the perfume she'd found at an exclusive boutique in Tuscany over the summer. She'd only been able to get away for a weekend and she'd had to work during the trip. Still, it wasn't so bad. That was simply the kind of sacrifice which ambitious people made.

Charlotte started the engine and drove up the ramp to the street. The new Jaguar purred. It was her first real car, the first one that indicated her status as a woman on her way to the top.

She turned the car in the direction Jake usually walked home. The car was cold from Grennan and Brennan's car park, which was arctic even in summer, and which was now frankly intolerable. Charlotte turned up the heater as she drove through the quiet streets.

The champagne made her light-headed. She hoped she wasn't pulled over and breathalysed. It was possible that she was over the legal limit.

Ahead, she saw a white Honda take a corner like a crazy person. Charlotte eased the Jag to a halt at the junction and watched the car shoot down the road to her right. Twenty, thirty feet away, she caught sight of Jake, talking to a woman on a bike.

The woman on the bike pushed off from the footpath. Charlotte held her breath and watched as the car ploughed straight into her, and screeched to a halt.

Liz got out of the car. She and Jake ran over to the woman. They seemed to argue. After a minute, they both got in Liz's car. It began reversing, moving in Charlotte's direction.

Charlotte put the Jag into reverse too. She eased it into a parking space at the side of the road, then killed the engine.

Liz's Honda stopped once it reached the crossroads. She changed direction and drove straight ahead, through a red light.

Unbelievable, Charlotte thought.

She watched as Liz's car stopped down the road. Jake got out, ran to the footpath. Was that a payphone he was using? They weren't sticking around, but they wanted to report the accident anonymously, Charlotte figured. As soon as Jake got back in the car, it sped away.

Charlotte started the Jag again, drove to where the woman lay on the road, and parked twenty feet away. She got out and made a quick assessment of the victim. A woman in her forties. Head trauma, possible trauma to the lower limbs. The woman was unconscious but still breathing.

"Hold on," Charlotte said. "Help is coming."

At least, she thought it was. She took out her phone and was about to call and make sure an ambulance was on its way when she heard a siren.

At least Jake had the decency to ring it in. But what was going on? Who was the woman? Charlotte noticed a notebook on the tarmac. Grabbing it, she looked at the first page.

Case notes: Jake Whelan.

She flicked through it with interest, decided she'd read it later.

The siren was close. Charlotte wondered whether to wait and tell the paramedics that Liz was responsible, that she and Jake had fled the scene. It would be a fitting punishment, but Charlotte was reluctant to stay when she had alcohol on her breath. And anyway, she had a better idea.

With the notebook in her hand, she hurried back to the Jag. She had only closed her door when the ambulance arrived, screeching to a halt next to the cyclist. Charlotte slowly eased away from the scene.

CHAPTER SEVEN

Jake's apartment was a tight one-bed, with a combined sitting room and kitchen. A tiny bathroom completed the setup. The paint was flaking off the walls in a couple of places near the windows.

Jake thought he'd be doing better by his early thirties. When he was studying law, he'd fantasised about million-euro yachts and three-month cruises on the Riviera – but here he was.

A job he hated, a girlfriend he wanted to dump, and an apartment barely big enough to house his stamp collection. Crazy high rent that devoured most of his income, retail therapy that pissed away the rest. No pension, no family, no time to catch up with friends.

And now this.

Jake walked to the kitchen. He turned the radio off and looked at Liz.

"You said Kathy was dead."

"I'm sure she was. I couldn't find a pulse." Liz shrugged. "I'm not sure. Maybe it was just weak."

"Liz." He shook his head.

"I'm sorry," she said. "I made a mistake. I was under a lot of pressure. But it's good, right?"

"We didn't have to flee the scene. We look like criminals."

Liz got to her feet and followed Jake to the kitchen area. She wrapped her arms around him. "You protected me. Thank you."

Jake said, "I should go to the hospital."

"Are you crazy? They'll think you're responsible."

"I am."

"We both are. But we'll be okay. We have to stay calm."

"I wonder if she'll wake up and remember I was there when it happened."

Liz said, "Did anyone know she was meeting you?"

"I don't think so."

"So let's see what happens. We don't know if she'll recover or not. Even if she's fine, she might not remember the crash."

"What if she does?"

"We'll deal with it." Liz gave him a shaky smile. "Right? We can handle anything together."

Jake felt a surge of guilt that he had thought of dumping her. He hugged Liz back. Together, they returned to the couch, which sat facing the microwave. Handy for when you wanted a snack, but otherwise not ideal.

"How long were you seeing this woman?"

"About a month."

"What for?"

"I just – I needed someone to talk to."

Liz's face fell. "You have me."

"Sure, but—"

"You think it's okay to cheat on me?"

Jake was startled by the venom in Liz's voice. Her face turned pink, her expression hardened.

"What do you mean?" Jake said. He forced a shaky laugh. "Kathy was my counsellor, my therapist. We talked. She was trying to help me."

"So that's fine, is it?"

"Why not? What do you mean?"

Liz sat on the couch as straight as a soldier. Her unblinking eyes stared into Jake's. A second ago, there had been warmth in those eyes. The sudden coldness unnerved him.

"I'm your girlfriend," Liz said. "You should talk to me."

"I do."

"But you needed more?"

He shook his head. "I don't know what you mean."

"Never mind."

Suddenly Liz was walking to the door.

Jake watched her. "Wait, where are you going?"

"I should wash the car. There might be blood on it. Your girlfriend's blood."

"She's my therapist!"

Liz stepped outside and slammed the door behind her. Jake heard her footfalls as she descended the stairs, her feet hitting each step as if it had personally insulted her. Then, the sound of the building's front door slamming.

What was that about?

Jake shook his aching head.

He really did want to go to the hospital, but he supposed Kathy would be in the operating room. Anyway, what right did he have to visit her? She'd taken time out of her holidays because he asked her, and this was her reward.

Jake walked over to the window and looked outside. The street outside was busier than the office district. People walked by, still in a festive mood. A mother and father swung a young girl between them, the child squealing with delight.

Jake thought of Kathy's husband, the kids she had mentioned. Did they know that she was in hospital? Should Jake contact them?

As he was thinking this, his phone buzzed with a text message.

Liz, for sure.

But it wasn't. The message was from Charlotte.

I want to see you in my office.

Fuck, Jake thought. She had been a partner two hours, and already she was trying to boss him around.

He tapped out a reply.

Sure. How about tomorrow after lunch?

His phone buzzed again with Charlotte's reply.

Now.

CHAPTER EIGHT

At Grennan and Brennan's offices, Jake swiped his card so he could pass through the turnstile next to the reception desk. He nodded to Fergal Long, a security guard who had worked at the company even longer than Jake had. Fergal was a taciturn man in his fifties with salt and pepper hair and a bad limp. He'd been a detective until an injury forced him into early retirement. His mind remained as sharp as ever though.

"Back again?" Fergal said.

"I was told to come in."

"We go where we're told, like the fellow said."

Fergal arrived at the office at six every evening. He watched the building until eight the following morning, maintaining himself on a diet of chocolate bars, soft drinks and cat videos, keeping his brain sharp by reading ancient Greek philosophy. He liked to hit young solicitors with brainteasers and words of wisdom.

Jake took the bait. "Who's the fellow that said that? Marcus Aurelius? Aristotle? Socrates?"

Fergal shrugged. "That one? I forget. Maybe that was me?"

Jake forced a smile and kept moving. Sometimes Fergal goofed around but Jake felt nervous being in the presence of a former detective. He felt like guilt was written on his own face for Fergal to read. In the elevator, Jake checked his watch. Only seven thirty, but it felt like midnight.

He stepped out of the elevator on the third floor. Most of his colleagues had gone home and large swathes of the office lay in darkness. What with Christmas, and the partnership announcement, everyone not hurrying home to their families had probably gone to the pub for some festive drinks. Charlotte's brightly lit office stood out.

Jake rapped his knuckles on the door and stepped inside. Charlotte was standing next to her bookshelf, leafing through a journal.

"You wanted to see me?"

Charlotte looked at him.

"Bring me the Kilvian Brewery files. I'm going to handle that from now on."

Jake's mouth fell open. Kilvian Brewery was a great client. He'd got the work through a friend of a friend and had been counting his blessings ever since. The company was riding the craft beer wave.

"What?" was all he could think to say. "Why?"

Charlotte smiled. "I'd like to give them my particular attention."

Jake would be in trouble without that work. Grennan and Brennan expected their employees to bring in cash, lots of it and often.

"You're working fast," Jake said.

"No point wasting time. Go get them."

He retrieved the paper files from his desk and brought them back. He wondered if this was symbolic. The digital file was already on the server for Charlotte to access. Maybe she wanted to humiliate him by making him hand over his paper copies. Well, if that was her intention, it was working. He felt undermined. He'd been just about to send the brewery an invoice, but he supposed Charlotte would take care of that now. He set the files down on her desk.

"Was there anything else?" he asked.

"Draft an e-mail to them for my approval, telling them I'll be their point of contact from now on."

"Draft an e-mail for your approval?" Jake snorted. "Like I'm your secretary?"

Charlotte walked across the room, stopping just in front of Jake. He caught the scent of her perfume.

She said, "How are the panic attacks?"

"What?"

"Better? Worse? Are you still crying as you walk to work in the mornings? Dreaming of throwing yourself in the canal but too chickenshit to do it?"

Jake flushed. "How did – where did you get that idea?"

"I have my sources," Charlotte said.

Jake had told no one at work about the panic attacks. Not even Liz. The only person on earth he'd told was Kathy.

Jake said, "I have no idea what you're getting at, but—"

"What did you buy Liz for Christmas?"

"Charlotte—"

"You should have given her some driving lessons."

Jake's heart hammered in his chest. "I have no idea—"

Charlotte said, "Don't play innocent. I know what you and your girlfriend did. Arthur wouldn't look kindly on employees carrying out hit-and-runs. It's considered bad form in the legal profession. Your careers would be over, of course, not that Liz was every going to amount to much. If the woman dies, Liz is looking at a charge of involuntary manslaughter. You'll go down for secondary participation."

Charlotte went over to her desk and picked up a notebook.

"Interesting reading. I had no idea you were so close to cracking."

After a moment, Jake realised what Charlotte held in her hands. Kathy's notes. The ones she'd dropped on the street before the accident. Charlotte must have been there, and seen what happened, must have come along afterwards and picked the notebook up.

Jake's mouth went dry.

Charlotte *knew*.

His life hung in her hands. Public shame, censure, long term unemployment, years in jail.

In a low voice he said, "Did you report it?"

"Not yet. But I can change that anytime. People are looking for you and Liz."

Jake made a grab for the notebook, but Charlotte pulled it out of his reach.

"Don't be stupid," she said with a laugh. "I have photos of these notes stored online."

"Are you joking me?"

"No, I'm not. It always pays to be careful. That's a lesson Liz could have done with."

Jake imagined Liz being taken away in cuffs. Her father, left alone, with no one to speak to, and no aide to speak through. It would kill him.

"Please don't report this," Jake said. "It was an accident."

"Why did you run then?"

"We thought she was dead. It was a mistake."

"Yes," Charlotte said, "It was a mistake, alright."

CHAPTER NINE

Liz parked under a lamppost in front of her building. The estate consisted of three blocks, each of them red brick, seven storeys tall, solid and neat. They'd been built in the seventies and occupied by countless young professionals since then, in the lonely years before starting a family. Liz knew that loneliness too well.

She had driven around the city for a long time, feeling uneasy. Feeling hurt, if she was honest. With the window open, she smoked cigarette after cigarette, ignoring the freezing air's bite, focusing instead on the nicotine rush. She'd more or less given up smoking, as Jake didn't like her tobacco breath.

Jake.

She couldn't understand him. He saw nothing wrong with opening up to some glorified agony aunt, while keeping his feelings a secret from her, his life partner. She wished he'd call. She had been sure he'd follow her when she stormed out of his apartment, but he hadn't. The important thing was to be together, especially at a time like this. But her phone had remained silent.

Liz stared at the closest apartment block, where she lived on the ground floor. This place was not ideal, but she wasn't able to afford luxury on a receptionist's salary – even a receptionist at a fancy law firm.

Soon things would change, though.

Liz and Jake would get married. She'd start studying. She'd become a lawyer too. She wasn't old, only thirty-four. There was time to start again.

Maybe have a couple of children.

Jake would make partner next year, no doubt about it, and their combined salaries would let them buy a house somewhere nice. They might not be able to afford Dublin, but one of the commuter towns in Kildare was probably within reach. She wouldn't mind commuting to work every day, only an hour or so each way, and she'd have her husband sitting next to her the whole way.

Liz had a smile on her face when she stepped out of the car.

She hit the key fob as a voice boomed out of the darkness.

"What's up?"

A figure was moving towards her across the lot. A tall man with powerful shoulders. He stepped into the light, eyes gleaming like a wolf's.

Liz recognised Colin McMahon. He lived on the floor above her and worked as a barista at Starbucks. He'd been flirting with her ever since she moved into the building. Asking her out, asking how she was, every time their paths crossed in the car park or the laundry room. She'd done nothing to encourage him, but even her thick-framed glasses hadn't put him off.

"Jesus, Colin, you scared the shit out of me."

He laughed. "Why are you so nervous?"

Liz shrugged. "Everywhere is so quiet. And then…"

"Boom! Yeah, I get it. Were you working today?"

"Yeah. You too?"

"Sure, have to keep the customers caffeinated."

Colin was a big, strong guy with a huge head and tiny impish eyes buried under V-shaped brows. She always thought he looked like he was halfway through transforming into a werewolf.

"Right." Liz swung her handbag over her shoulder. "I better be going."

"What happened to your car?"

Liz's muscles tensed.

"What do you mean?"

Colin walked around the front.

"The scratch there? And the bump? The bonnet's a little dented. Not to mention… that looks like blood."

Liz's mouth dropped open. "What? Where?"

Colin pointed. "There and there and there."

Fuck. He was right. Liz saw red smears of blood.

"Oh, that. I hit a deer."

"A deer?" Colin's eyes widened. "Where? Got a better chance of winning the lottery than hitting a deer in Dublin."

"Lucky me, I guess."

Liz swallowed. She hadn't expected a cross-examination, but it had been stupid to park under the light.

"I'm going inside," she said. "It's cold."

Colin reached out, gripped her arm above the elbow and held it tight.

He said, "Well, it's funny, but I was listening to the news as I drove home. I heard about an accident. A hit-and-run."

"Oh?"

"You didn't hear? I guess you were too busy driving through deer country. Where is that, by the way? Deer country?"

"Um…"

Colin shook his head like it didn't matter.

"Funny. I usually remember where I was ten minutes ago. But maybe I'm strange. Anyhow, the news—"

"Let go of me."

Colin looked at his hand as if he'd forgotten he was holding her. He let go, loosening each finger theatrically.

She set off walking away from him.

"That news show," Colin called after her. "The one I heard, they said someone knocked a lady down. In the south inner city. That's where you work, isn't it?"

Liz said, "So what?"

"So nothing. I just thought you might want to drink a beer with me. We could have a chat. Unwind after a long day."

"I don't think so. I have things to do."

She kept walking.

"I just hope you don't get in any trouble," Colin said.

Liz stopped, turned around. Colin had an infuriatingly smug look on his face.

"Come again?" Liz said.

"If someone saw all that blood on your car, they might get the wrong idea. Think you had something to do with that hit-and-run that happened near your office."

Did he really suspect her? It was such rotten luck that he had seen the car. Liz couldn't risk ending up in jail, having Jake end up in jail. She couldn't let anything keep them apart. Maybe she needed to play Colin's game.

Liz said, "That's the worst chat-up line I've ever heard."

"Sorry. I'm not very smooth. My brain shoots around from topic to topic. I just thought we could chill out and have a beer. Relax after a long day, right?"

"I guess I am thirsty. One beer?"

"Or wine if you like. I have wine too."

"At your place?"

"Sure. I'm not driving anywhere."

Liz said, "Alright. A drink might help me unwind."

Colin caught up with her and took her hand in his. So they were going to pretend he wasn't blackmailing her. Liz resisted the urge to pull away. She was in trouble. That was for sure. But she had no idea know how much.

CHAPTER TEN

Colin's apartment was on the first floor, almost directly above Liz's. She wondered what his place was like. Maybe the walls were painted black, a cross hung upside-down on the wall and the sink was piled high with festering dishes. She braced herself as he unlocked his door.

As she stepped inside, she realised it wasn't so bad. The apartment was bare, with pale blue walls and a few pieces of furniture from Ikea.

"Let me give you the tour," Colin said as he closed the door. He paused a second and said, "Well, I hope you enjoyed the tour."

The apartment's layout was similar to that of her own place. The front door led into a small sitting room. A corridor led to a tiny bedroom, a kitchen and a bathroom.

"You live alone?"

"Sure," Colin said. "Is it like your place?"

"A bit."

"I'd like to see that for myself sometime."

Liz coughed so she wouldn't have to answer. Colin was never getting inside her apartment. That was for sure.

The main feature in the sitting room was a huge TV. Underneath it lay a PlayStation and two controllers. A square table with a laptop and speakers sat in the corner.

Colin hung his jacket on the back of a chair and powered up the laptop.

The car, Liz thought.

She had to get back to it before someone else noticed the signs of an accident.

"Red or white? I have a little of both left over from Christmas."

It took Liz a moment to realise he was talking about wine. "Actually, I'd like a beer."

Colin nodded with approval. "A beer-drinking chick? Alright, I like it."

He went into the kitchen. Liz heard the sound of a fridge opening.

"The building's so quiet," Liz said. Colin came back and handed her a bottle. No glass. Cap still on.

"Good, isn't it?"

"I think it's kind of creepy."

Colin used a bottle opener on his keyring to pop his own bottle's cap, then sank down on one side of the couch. Perhaps out of habit, he glanced at the TV.

"Sit down," he said.

Liz did, leaving a space between them, but Colin scooted nearer to her. She accepted the bottle opener from him. After popping the cap, she looked around for somewhere to put it.

"Just throw it on the floor," Colin said.

"Are you nuts? I can't do that."

"I don't own the place."

"Doesn't matter."

Colin took a swig of beer. "Do you have OCD?"

Liz went to the kitchen, where she found the bin. She also found a knife block on the kitchen counter. Five knife handles stuck out of the wood. Solid steel, judging by the look of them.

Liz reached out for the nearest knife. Her fingers had just touched the cold handle when heavy metal music filled the air at a deafening volume. A raging wall of distorted guitars, pounding bass and thundering drums.

Liz took a breath to steady herself.

She threw the bottle cap into the bin and returned to the sitting room. Colin was leaning over his laptop. He glanced at her over his shoulder.

"Alright?"

He turned the speaker up louder.

Colin couldn't have been less like Jake. Jake, with his Beethoven and his Handel and, when he really went wild, jazz. Liz felt a headache coming on.

"Could you turn it down a little?"

"What?"

She gestured downwards with her hand.

"What?" Colin said, with a hand to his ear.

Liz leaned in. "I said, could you—"

Colin turned down the music. Then he grabbed her. Got in her face. His stubble scratched her chin as he found her mouth and pressed his tongue inside.

She tried to pull away, but he held her in place. With an urgency that startled her, Colin pressed his body against her.

His disgusting tongue probed her mouth, his saliva mingling with her own. He towered over her, huge and powerful.

Liz gagged.

Colin only stopped kissing her when Liz bit his tongue hard enough to draw blood.

She followed that up by driving her knee into his crotch.

He doubled over and his face turned purple.

"Fucking bitch," he wheezed.

Tiny droplets of blood flew out of his mouth when he spoke.

Liz wondered if she had time to get to the knives, or if he'd kill her before she reached the kitchen.

CHAPTER ELEVEN

Jake's throat went dry as he gazed at Charlotte, who had the power to ruin Liz's life and his too, if he wasn't careful.

"So let me get this straight," Jake said. "You're not going to tell anyone what happened, but you're going to hold this over me forever? That's what you're telling me?"

Charlotte smiled. "I'm simply telling you where you stand."

"Which is nowhere."

"I thought you'd understand," Charlotte said. "I expect that ten thousand euro to be in my bank account by the end of the week."

Jake swallowed.

"I don't have it," he said. He had no way to get it either, unless the bank was willing to give him a loan.

Charlotte sat down behind her desk and turned her attention to her computer. She said, "You better figure out how to get it. By the way, did you know you're being paid significantly less than other associates?"

"How do you know that? Is that true?"

"It's true."

"Why?" He felt a surge of outrage.

"I'll let you think about it for yourself. Now go home."

Like a beaten dog, Jake dragged himself out of her office and headed for the bank of elevators. The whole evening felt a nightmare. Being passed over for promotion, the car crash, and now Charlotte blackmailing Jake into doing whatever she wanted… forever.

She could boss him around, and there would be nothing he could do. Not if he and Liz wanted to stay out of jail.

Jake's life had gone into free-fall.

What was he going to do?

His stomach roiled.

Maybe what she'd said about backing up Kathy's notebook online was a bluff. Maybe not. Charlotte was meticulous. Jake wouldn't have dreamt of hurting her anyway. He didn't want his therapist's case notes to be revealed, but he would never have thought of hurting Charlotte to stop that happening. The last time Jake had been in a physical fight, he'd been about five years old. He didn't possess that killer instinct some of his colleagues seemed to have. He just wanted to have a quiet life.

Jake was still thinking when he walked straight into Arthur Grennan.

The managing partner appeared out of nowhere in the corridor. Jake ploughed into him, knocking the old man on his backside.

Grennan let out a gasp of pain as he crumpled on the floor.

"Jesus, Arthur, I'm sorry."

"You *idiot*."

Jake flinched at the rebuke, but he helped Grennan to his feet.

"Are you okay? I'm so sorry."

"Look where you're going."

"I didn't know anyone else was here."

"What are you doing here?"

"I was just… I was getting a file for Charlotte."

Grennan snorted. Jake could almost read his mind. *Getting files is all you're good for.*

Jake said nothing as the old man hobbled past him, down the corridor.

"Shit," Jake whispered.

He pressed the button for the elevator and stepped inside.

Going down.

CHAPTER TWELVE

Liz sprinted down Colin's hallway, through the open doorway into the kitchen. The knife block was on the counter. She threw herself at it as Colin staggered after her. She could feel his breath on the back of her neck, could smell the beer on his breath. His hand slapped against the doorjamb behind her as he struggled for purchase.

"Come back here," he snarled.

Liz's hands were clumsy, fumbling with one knife handle and then another. She glanced over her shoulder and saw Colin advancing on her, breathing hard. An expression of blind rage spread over his face. He seemed to have grown two feet taller since he got mad. She wasn't going to be able to sweet-talk her way out of this one.

She finally got a grip on the biggest knife in the block at the same time that Colin grabbed her shoulder, pulling her around.

As she turned, she lashed out, stabbing at Colin.

He grunted when she nicked his chin.

Liz lunged forward again, knife first. Colin grabbed the blade with his fingers, and Liz forced the sharp edge down, cutting deeper into his flesh, drawing a howl of agony from Colin's mouth. She pulled the blade away, then lashed out again.

It sliced through the air, hitting nothing, but Colin jerked backwards to avoid the blade. His head smashed hard into the doorframe.

Thank god, Liz thought.

A moment of surprise, of disorientation.

She lost no time throwing herself at him. But she wasn't fast enough. Colin saw her coming and thrust a massive fist at her. It hit her arm, just above the wrist. The knife fell from her fingers, clattering on the kitchen tiles. Liz fell on her backside.

At once, Colin was on top of her, pinning her down.

"Let me up."

"You fucking cut me."

"I said, let me up."

He gave her an appraising look.

"I didn't believe you did that hit-and-run. I was only playing. Now I'm not so sure."

"I don't care what you think."

"Now I can believe it. I can believe you—"

"I said I don't care, asshole."

He slapped her across the face with the back of his hand, knocking her glasses onto the floor. The world blurred.

"Shut your bitch mouth."

He unbuckled his belt and pulled it out of the loops in his jeans. Liz watched him, a roaring sound filling her ears.

"You know why I'm going to enjoy this?" Colin undid the button on his jeans and began to zip his fly down. "Because you're going to see that you're no better than I am. Oh, I know, you walk around like you're so great. Not anymore."

He was smiling, confident that he was in charge. He didn't realise Liz had another blade. Not as sharp as the kitchen knife, but sharp enough.

She worked her hand into the pocket of her jacket slowly, and clasped Jake's Swiss Army knife. She waited until Colin shifted his weight, so he could wriggle one leg out of his jeans, and then she pulled out the knife.

Colin saw it. Saw Liz's other hand reach over and pull the blade open.

His eyes widened, but he was off-balance.

Liz stabbed it into Colin's thigh as hard as she could.

He howled like a pig. Liz shoved him off her. She was on her feet in a second, scooping up her glasses and putting them on, looking around for something, anything, to defend herself with.

Colin was already pushing himself up from the tiles.

A meat tenderiser caught Liz's eye. It was a mean-looking hammer with dozens of sharp metal points. Good for pounding dumb meat.

Liz grabbed it off the counter. Turning, she smashed it into the side of Colin's head.

He went down without a sound.

Liz slumped on the floor next to him.

Her breathing was ragged, her ears pulsing with blood, its flow as fast as the heavy metal music had been.

She sat on the floor with her legs crossed, willing her breathing to return to normal. Once its frantic pace had slowed, Liz glanced at the mess around her.

The unconscious man.

The blood.

This is going to be hard to explain, she thought.

Then the doorbell rang.

CHAPTER THIRTEEN

After Jake left, Charlotte decided to stay at the office to get more work done. As a new partner, there was much to do, though of course she had been preparing for this day for years.

When she went to the canteen to grab a coffee, she saw Arthur Grennan.

He was stalking the corridors like a vulture, muttering to himself, his face pink, his lips cracked from the cold air. Charlotte thought it best to stay out of his way.

The canteen was closed, but she slipped behind the counter to make herself a coffee.

As the water boiled, Charlotte thought of the tantalising rumour her father had told her. Soon the government would appoint Arthur as a High Court judge. He'd have to give up his job in the firm in order to accept the position. If that happened, Charlotte was confident she'd be able to take over as managing partner.

She brought her coffee back to her desk. This was the last night she'd sit in this chair. Tomorrow morning a larger office would await, with "CHARLOTTE FLYNN, PARTNER" emblazoned across the door.

As she took a sip of coffee, her phone rang. It was her mother.

"Sorry for disturbing you, Charlotte. Can you talk?"

"Yes, it's fine. I did it. I made partner."

"Of course, you did, Charlotte. We knew you'd be successful."

Charlotte smiled. "I thought so, but you can never be sure."

"And what about that fellow you work with? How disappointed was he?"

Charlotte pictured Jake standing up when her name was called. The pained look on his face as he hurried from the conference room.

"Very disappointed," she said. "But that's nothing to do with me. Jake didn't earn it."

"Don't you still like him? Are you going to ask him out?"

Thump.

Charlotte remembered the sound of Liz's car smashing into the therapist's body. Then she pictured Jake in her office a few minutes earlier. The pathetic look on his face.

She couldn't believe she'd ever thought he might make a desirable partner. The prospect was laughable.

"Things have become complicated," Charlotte said.

"Yes, well, maybe he isn't the right type anyway. Not enough fire in his belly."

"That's true," Charlotte said.

Or maybe he just hasn't learnt to kindle it yet.

"On the other hand," her mother said, "remember Lucy Reynolds. You know how much I love Lucy. She's my best friend, after all, but she was alone all her life because she was so fussy. No one was ever good enough."

"I'm not fussy. But I have standards."

"You sound just like Lucy."

"No, I don't."

"Lucy is so lonely now that she's retired. All she does these days is collect ceramic figurines. It's deranged. You know what I've always loved about your father?"

Charlotte sighed. "Yes."

"It bears repeating. I've always loved him because he has a kind heart. Even if he is a politician. Most people might not even believe he has a heart. But you know how he is. Beneath that hard-as-nails facade, he's a big sweetie."

"I know." Charlotte's tone was sharper than she'd meant. "I know," she said more gently.

"There's a lot you can forgive a good man."

Not mutilating a Givenchy coat, Charlotte thought.

"I need to get back to work," she said, ending the call.

There was a meeting tomorrow she needed to prepare for, and it shouldn't take more than three or four hours. This was why Charlotte was made partner and Jake was not. He was not willing to do the unpleasant things that sometimes had to be done.

CHAPTER FOURTEEN

Jake got on a number 7 bus, headed for St. Vincent's Hospital. Unable to face going home, he hoped he might be able to get some news about Kathy's condition if he went to the hospital.

He took a seat at the back, next to a sullen teenage boy in a puffy black jacket and grey tracksuit bottoms. The boy's hair was skin-tight at the back and sides and sprouting like a vegetable from the top of his head. His phone blared. Music and snatches of video clips. The only other person on the lower deck was an old woman huddled up at a window seat halfway down the bus.

At least the bus was warm. Jake could feel hot air blasting from the vents behind him. He had waited twenty minutes in the freezing cold.

Jake wasn't sure what he'd do if Kathy was not alright. He stared out the window feeling more wretched than ever before.

Beside him, the boy was now talking loudly on the phone. Normally Jake would have done nothing, just tolerated the selfish behaviour, but he was so far outside of his comfort zone right now, the boundary lines were a blur.

"Hey, be quiet," Jake said.

The teenager gave him a look. He said, "Fuck off," then turned away.

Rage boiled up inside Jake's brain.

"No, fuck you," Jake snapped. He grabbed the phone and smashed it against the handrail. There was a crunch of glass on metal as the screen broke. Jake turned and flipped open the window. The boy grabbed him from behind, but Jake ignored him and lobbed the phone out the window.

"No one wants to hear your shit," he said, closing the window.

The boy put his hands to his head and said, "You bollocks."

Jake formed a fist and hit the boy once in the mouth, his knuckles closed tight and his arm straight, the way he'd been taught in karate class when he was a kid.

The boy tumbled onto the floor, probably more surprised than hurt, uttered a muffled threat, then ran to the front of the bus, where he shouted at the driver. But the bus kept going until the next stop. As soon as the door opened, the teenager jumped out.

Jake flashed the boy the finger as he walked past the window. He saw with satisfaction that a few drops of blood coloured his lips.

Jake leaned back in his seat as the bus started moving again. A warm feeling of satisfaction filled him. The old woman had turned in her seat and looked at Jake.

"Sorry about that," he said.

The woman turned away without a word.

The happy feeling stayed with Jake until the bus approached the hospital. He pressed the button and walked to the front of the bus.

"Nice one," the driver said, giving Jake a wink as the door opened.

Jake wondered how often the driver had wanted to give some unruly passenger a punch.

He stepped off the bus, onto a deserted footpath. Various hospital buildings loomed out of the darkness on the other side of the road.

He crossed at the pedestrian lights, which took him to the shopping centre beside the hospital. Then he waited to cross the next road, over to the hospital.

His phone began to ring as he stood there. The screen said, "LIZ CALLING". He put it back in his pocket without answering, as the light turned green for him to cross the road.

He made his way up a stone path to the main hospital building, past a few hardy smokers, and through the electric doors. Light and heat hit him at the same time.

He stepped in front of a passing nurse, a young Indian woman.

"I'm looking for Dr. Katherine O'Brien. She was the victim of a hit-and-run."

The young woman nodded. "Are you family?"

"No. I'm a friend."

She pulled Jake out of the way of a passing stretcher.

"I'm afraid you can't see her now."

"I know it's late. I'm sorry. But I'm a good friend. Can you tell me anything?"

The nurse sighed.

"The patient came out of surgery ten minutes ago, but she has not regained consciousness."

"Is she okay?"

The nurse spoke slowly. "We will have to assess her condition when she wakes up. All we can say for now is that she is stable."

Jake nodded.

"Thank you," he said.

At least Kathy was alive.

So far.

CHAPTER FIFTEEN

Liz slipped her phone in her pocket. She really needed to talk to Jake but he wasn't answering. She stood in the doorway of Colin's kitchen and listened.

The doorbell rang again.

Colin was unconscious, flat on his back on the floor. He hadn't moved since she hit him on the side of the head with the meat-tenderiser.

Was he breathing?

She was afraid to check.

Afraid he'd reach out and grab her.

She crept to the door and peered through the peephole. Two young men were standing in the corridor. Rough-looking men. Each of them was carrying a six-pack of beer. Friends of Colin? He hadn't mentioned anything about having friends over, but that didn't mean much. The thought of getting Liz into his apartment might have swept everything else out of his mind.

One of the men stepped forward and banged on the door.

"Hey Colin? Open up, man."

Liz watched through the glass as the other guy pulled out a phone.

As quietly as she could, she made her way back to the kitchen, just as Colin's phone began to ring. The ring tone was like an old-fashioned telephone.

Brrring, Brrring.

It was coming from somewhere on Colin. She crouched down. The phone had to be in his jeans, which were bundled around his knees. Her fingers shook as she slipped them into the right front pocket.

Nothing there but a ball of snotty tissues, all wet and squishy.

Colin emitted a soft moan. She waited to see if he would move.

The phone continued ringing.

Brrring, Brrring.

Its sound was muffled, but she needed to silence it before the men outside heard. She hoped they would go away. But if Colin had invited them to his place, they'd wonder what had happened to him, why he wasn't answering.

Liz slipped her hand into Colin's other pocket. She found the phone straight away, wedged in next to his wallet. Liz pulled the phone out and rejected the incoming call.

She turned the phone off.

Hopefully Colin's friends would get bored and leave.

"Uuhhh…"

Colin moaned softly.

His arm twitched.

If he called for help, she was done for. They'd burst in and see what she'd done. The three of them would gang-rape Liz and kill her. She had no doubt about it. Colin seemed like that kind of guy, and his friends looked the same.

She opened the kitchen drawers one by one, looking for anything useful. She found a ball of twine in the second drawer. It would have to do. In the same drawer, she found a pair of nail scissors.

Liz needed a gag too.

She opened the cupboard under the sink. A foul-looking dish cloth sat on a soap dish. Liz didn't want to touch the cloth, but she forced herself to pick it up.

She brought everything over to the place on the floor where Colin lay sprawled. He looked awful in the unforgiving glare of the fluorescent light. Waxy, like a corpse laid out for viewing.

She crouched down and tied his ankles together, hoping he was still too out-of-it to notice. Once his legs were secure, she moved onto his hands.

She knew she'd have to be fast, in case he felt her tying him up.

Liz took a breath, then set to work, bringing the two wrists together and wrapping the twine around them.

She'd made only a couple of passes when Colin coughed and pulled his hands apart.

He was waking up.

Outside, his friends banged on the door again.

She pulled Colin's hands together again and held them with one hand while running circles of twine around them with the other.

Colin's eyes fluttered open. He blinked at Liz.

She finished tying a knot just as he realised what she was doing to him.

He opened his mouth wide to scream, to call for help – and Liz shoved the dish cloth into his mouth, muffling his screams.

He still managed to make too much noise though. Liz pushed the cloth in deeper.

"Quiet," she said.

Colin glared at her, his face turning purple.

Liz stood up. Jake's pen knife still stuck out of Colin's thigh. She'd stuck him with it pretty nice. She yanked the knife out. Colin jerked and his muffled screaming became more intense. Liz stepped aside and watched him.

What a waste of energy.

He couldn't go anywhere.

She walked to front door and looked through the peephole. Colin's friends were walking away.

Relieved, Liz slumped on the couch, exhausted after the ordeal. She needed a moment to cool off. Good thing she'd taken Jake's penknife. It had come in handy, not only for slicing up Charlotte's dress but for sticking that piece of shit in the kitchen.

Liz wondered what Jake was doing.

She hoped Charlotte wasn't going to start throwing her weight around now that she was a partner. Liz wasn't about to let anyone keep Jake away from her.

CHAPTER SIXTEEN

Leaving the hospital, Jake couldn't help feeling dispirited. But at least Kathy had not died. He walked through the automatic doors and stepped outside, immediately finding himself swallowed by the dark night.

Jake crossed the road to the supermarket. He walked the aisles aimlessly. The growling of his stomach reminded him he was hungry, yet he couldn't decide what to eat. In the end, he left without buying anything.

He set off walking towards home, gazing blankly at the huge houses he passed. Charlotte would one day live in this kind of neighbourhood. With a Maserati parked behind an electric gate. CCTV cameras and a fancy security system to protect her.

This place wasn't for Jake.

I used to think I was smart.

But he had been wrong. Being passed over for partner again was evidence of that. The hit-and-run was more. Not only was he stupid, but he was a coward.

I've turned into a shitty person, Jake thought.

But when? And how had it happened?

His phone buzzed. Liz was calling.

No hello when he picked up. She said, "I need you, Jake."

"Liz, I feel sick."

"What? Where are you?"

"I went to the hospital."

"What's wrong with you?" Liz sounded almost hysterical.

"I went to check on Kathy but they wouldn't let me see her."

"Are you crazy? Don't go near that woman. Look, I need you to come to my place. We have another problem."

Jake frowned. He couldn't imagine how things might get any worse. He didn't even want to know.

"Okay," he said. "I'm on my way."

As he hung up the phone, his stomach rumbled again. Ignoring it, he changed course, walking towards Liz's place.

It took twenty minutes to get there, walking through the dark streets. When he passed a family, perhaps walking home from the shops or from visiting family, their high spirits just about broke his heart. Two adults and two kids. A perfect little family.

Soon he reached Liz's road. He ducked into the entrance to her estate, saw three large blocks of apartments ahead. Jake realised his fingers were numb. He'd forgotten to wear gloves, a hat or a scarf.

And the jacket he was wearing was too light for this weather.

He set off across the car park towards the building.

"Jake?"

He turned towards the sound. Liz was walking towards him, carrying a bucket in one hand. She looked awful. Haggard and tired, as if she had aged ten years during the day.

He said, "What are you doing?"

"I needed to wash the car."

"Why did you need to…"

Because of the blood, he realised.

Kathy's DNA was on the car, and Liz was cleaning away the evidence of their crime. That must be why she wanted him there. To help her. Or so he would be complicit in this too. They were bound together by this accident.

Liz said, "I'll need to get the dents fixed too, but—"

His stomach heaved at the thought of Kathy's blood splashed across the white paintwork.

Liz said, "Are you okay?"

Jake nodded, though his mouth was flooding with saliva. He hurried over to the strip of grass behind the cars and vomited in the grass.

He stayed bent over, waiting to see if he would be sick again. And he was. Another spurt of vomit shot from his mouth just as Liz reached him and put a hand on his back.

"I'm sorry," Jake said, straightening up. "I have to go."

"What?"

Jake didn't wait for an answer. He turned away and set off walking briskly in the direction he had just come from. He ignored Liz when she called his name.

CHAPTER SEVENTEEN

Liz's throat tightened as she watched Jake hurry across the car park. He couldn't leave her alone. She needed him.

"Jake? Wait."

"I'm sorry," he muttered, without looking back.

She ran after him, catching up with him as he reached the street, grabbing his arm at the elbow.

"Jake."

He shook off her hand without looking.

"Sorry, Liz. I can't do this right now."

He set off down the road. The chill air suddenly felt colder. Only the plastic bucket Liz held in one hand was remotely warm, from the warm water she'd used to wash her car. To wash the blood away.

She understood Jake being emotional. He was a sensitive man. But she was in trouble. She needed him.

She thought of the *Good luck* card she had given him. *To Jake, my partner.*

They were in this together.

She hadn't been given a chance to tell him that Colin knew their secret. She really wanted Jake's help to figure out what to do about that, but it seemed she'd have to handle it on her own.

She walked back the way she had come, passing her car and entering the apartment building. She got the elevator to Colin's floor, and let herself into his apartment.

Colin still lay tied up and gagged on the kitchen floor. When he saw her, he tried to speak. She stepped over him and began to fill up the bucket with more hot water.

"Are you calm?" Liz asked.

Colin glared at her in reply. He was a sorry sight, with his pants around his ankles and blood running down his legs from where she'd stabbed him. A trickle of blood ran down the side of his head from when she had hit him with the meat tenderiser. The floor tiles were smeared with blood. Liz was relieved that the twine at his ankles and wrists had held strong.

Maybe she could talk to him now. They might be able to reason this out, like two sensible adults. Something unfortunate had happened, but that didn't mean they couldn't move past it.

She hunkered down and pulled the dish cloth out of his mouth.

"You fucking stupid bitch. I'm gonna fucking kill you, you—"

"Let's talk about this calmly, okay?"

"You're so fucking dead. I'm gonna rip your stupid head off and shit down your neck."

Colin's face turned an apoplectic shade of purple. A vein bulged at the side of his forehead.

She shoved the cloth back in his mouth.

Liz said, "I give you one chance, and that's what you say to me? You threaten me? Use crude language and insult me? You're the stupid one."

Colin jerked his head from side to side and thrashed around with his body. He grunted loudly. Too loudly.

Liz waited until he'd stopped moving around so much. Then she grabbed his head with one hand and, with the other, she shoved the gag in deeper.

She walked over to the sink, where the bucket was overflowing with water, turned off the tap and lifted the bucket. It was heavy, but she had to carry it.

Panting and fighting for breath, her arms aching, Liz brought the bucket out to the car and emptied the hot water over the bonnet. Then she moved the car to a darker corner of the car park. She'd like to avoid letting people see the dent, if she could.

When she was done, she brought the empty bucket back upstairs to Colin's place.

He didn't move or make a sound this time, even when Liz set the bucket down on the floor next to his face.

"Are you calm?" she asked again. She wondered if it was worth trying to reason with him one more time.

She hunkered down and slapped Colin's face.

He wasn't calm.

He was dead.

CHAPTER EIGHTEEN

The next morning, Jake arrived at the office feeling like a zombie. The two cups of coffee he'd drank as he stood in his kitchen couldn't compensate for the lack of sleep. He'd been awake all night, hoping that Kathy would pull through.

Liz had called him twenty-seven times. He ignored her. Judging by the times of the phone calls, she didn't sleep either.

As he pushed through the gleaming glass doors of Grennan and Brennan, he caught sight of her sitting behind the reception desk. She had bags under her bloodshot eyes, but was smartly dressed and had done full make-up as usual. The lobby was empty. She leaned forward when she saw him.

"We need to talk," Liz hissed.

"Later," Jake said. "I'm going to call the hospital. I was waiting until a reasonable hour. Now should be okay."

"Jake."

"I said, later, Liz."

It seemed like everyone wanted to push Jake around and he was getting sick of it.

Jake saw Charlotte in her office. She was absorbed in something on her computer screen. He hurried past her office to his own.

Once there, he closed the door and slumped in his chair. He picked up the desk phone and phoned St. Vincent's. The call was transferred to a nurses' station.

"I was hoping to find out how Dr. Katherine O'Brien is doing."

A woman with an Indian accent answered. "Are you family?"

"No."

"I can't tell you anything if you are not family."

"I'm her friend. I visited last night."

A pause.

Please, Jake thought.

"The good friend?"

"That's right," he said. "I think you and I talked briefly. What's your name?"

"Shilpa."

"I'm sorry to bother you, Shilpa, but I'm really worried about Dr. O'Brien. I was up all night thinking about her. Can you just tell me if she's got better or worse?"

"She woke up an hour ago," Shilpa whispered.

Jake broken out in a huge grin. "That's fantastic," he said.

"She is not out of the woods yet, but she is doing better."

"Wonderful. Thank you so much. Thank you, Shilpa."

"You're welcome."

It was like a crushing weight had been lifted. Jake had been sure Kathy would die or stay in a coma. It was a massive relief to hear she was improving. Liz would be delighted.

Jake hurried out of his office.

He took the elevator back down to reception.

Two young men in jeans and hoodies were sitting on the couches in front of the reception desk. They looked like college students who'd got lost. One was thin, with straggly long hair and round glasses. The other was pink faced, with brown hair cut so uniformly short that he resembled a kiwi. Jake wondered if they were the children of one of his colleagues.

He walked over to Liz, who had her phone to her ear. She hung up when she saw him.

"I was trying to call you."

"Amazing news, Liz. She's woken up."

"Who?"

"Kathy, of course. I spoke to a nurse."

"Is she talking?"

Jake said, "I don't know. I don't think so. But she's improving. Isn't that great?"

Liz sighed. "We need to talk. Urgently."

"Okay. Now?"

"Now would be best. But those gentlemen are here to see you."

Liz nodded towards the young men on the couch.

Jake whispered, "Who are they?"

"They're from LoveBugg."

"LoveBugg? What the hell is that?"

"The dating app."

A vague memory stirred within Jake. A phone call before Christmas. A Gary or a Gareth. He asked for a meeting, but was shy on details. They'd arranged a date and afterwards Jake forgot all about it. He supposed the appointment was in his diary, but he hadn't checked it.

Liz said, "The one who looks like he belongs in a 70s metal band is the CFO, Fran Duggan. The one who looks like a solider on leave is Gareth Reynolds, the CEO."

"They don't look old enough to run a lemonade stand."

"Find me after your meeting," Liz hissed. "It's extremely important."

"Okay, okay."

Jake walked over to the couch.

"Good morning," he said, extending his hand. "I'm Jake Whelan."

Gareth got to his feet and grasped Jake's hand. His grip was firm. A downy fuzz coated his upper lip.

"How's it going?" Gareth said. He had a quick smile and deep brown eyes. Perceptive eyes. "You forgot we were coming, didn't you?"

"Yes," Jake admitted. He was probably the only person in the building who would have said that. "I had no memory of it whatsoever."

Gareth laughed. "I like your candour."

He shook hands with Fran too. With his lean face and round glasses, he looked like the definition of a nerd.

"Come on," Jake said. "Let's see if a conference room is free."

The two young men followed behind, looking every bit like a couple of work experience students.

CHAPTER NINETEEN

At half past nine, Charlotte was walking past Conference Room 3 when she happened to see Jake and two young men through the glass wall.

She recognised Gareth Reynolds from LoveBugg at once. Charlotte knew the CEO of every significant company.

The second man looked familiar. Beneath his head-banger's hair, his face was thoughtful. He had the shrewd expression of a quant. Probably the company's finance whizz.

A quiver of excitement passed through Charlotte. A rumour was circulating – within a very exclusive circle – that LoveBugg had been offered a generous sum by one of the big tech companies, in return for a 49% stake in the company. This could be an excellent opportunity to get the work. Charlotte assumed that this must be an exploratory meeting.

She pushed open the door to the conference room. Jake was saying, "Alright, let's begin."

It sounded like he was talking to himself rather than to the others. Charlotte saw right away that something had changed with Jake. He didn't look like the mess he had the previous day.

Charlotte cleared her throat. She said, "You weren't going to start without me, were you?"

The three men turned to Charlotte.

Gareth said, "I didn't realise we were having company."

He seemed annoyed to be interrupted, even by someone who looked as good as Charlotte.

Jake stood up. "Sorry, guys. Let me introduce you. Charlotte Flynn is head of mergers and acquisitions here. Would you like to join us, Charlotte?"

Gareth held up his hands in a *stop* gesture.

"No offence," he said. "But I figure finding one honest lawyer is rare enough. I don't want to push my luck."

Firm tone. Good insight. Impressive in someone so young, Charlotte thought. She let the door fall shut behind her.

"I work closely with Jake," Charlotte said. "I think you'll find my input valuable."

"We want to keep this between as few people as possible. We're talking about a sensitive matter."

Charlotte took her time, walking the length of the room. She stopped next to Gareth.

"Who made you the offer? Microsoft or Google? Or both?"

Gareth's head bounced back like he'd been punched.

"Where the hell did you get that?"

Charlotte smiled. "I heard about it weeks ago. I imagine they valued LoveBugg at about €125-175 million."

Now it was the turn of the long-haired man to look flummoxed.

He glowered at Charlotte. "The figures are confidential. Where did you hear that?"

"You must be Fran?"

"Yeah."

"I came up with the valuation myself. It's only an estimate, using a two-stage discounted cash flow model. I like to have a ballpark figure. Is the real number in that range?"

The two men exchanged a look.

Gareth gave a barely perceptible nod.

Fran sighed. He said, "€160 million. They told us not to tell anyone."

A surge of satisfaction washed over Charlotte, though she made sure not to let them see it.

Jake cleared his throat. "Charlotte is the best lawyer I've ever met. She knows what she's talking about, so I suggest you let her sit in and listen to her advice. Frankly it will be better than mine. Or anyone else's, for that matter."

"Fine," Gareth said. "You can stay."

Charlotte sat down. This deal could bring Grennan and Brennan huge fees, the kind that would make Arthur Grennan forget about firing Jake.

She soon had the measure of the two men. As expected, Gareth Reynolds was the visionary. Fran Duggan was the number-cruncher They were both a year out of college. The only surprise was that they had finished their degrees.

Charlotte took control of the meeting, both because she was better informed than Jake and to show Jake that she was the boss. She also wanted to establish herself as the face of the firm with LoveBugg. If things played out as Charlotte expected, she could be billing these guys for years.

As the meeting went on, Charlotte realised that Jake had built rapport with Gareth and Fran. They turned to him for confirmation of things Charlotte said. Though he barely gave a word of legal value, they believed he was a straight-shooter, and that could be valuable.

When the meeting was over, Charlotte and Jake rode down in the elevator with Gareth and Fran, and saw them to the door, where they shook hands and said their goodbyes. Charlotte was confident that she and Jake would get the work.

She was watching the two men walk away when Jake said, "I need to talk to Liz."

Charlotte was aware of Liz watching them. The receptionist looked like death, so clearly something was wrong. On the other hand, Jake seemed carefree.

Charlotte wondered if someone had found out about the hit-and-run. Maybe Jake didn't know yet. Or didn't care, for some reason.

Interesting.

Charlotte sensed two paths diverging.

"No," Charlotte said. "You can't talk to Liz. Come to my office. Now."

CHAPTER TWENTY

Charlotte's office was getting more cluttered, what with all the extra work she was taking on, but soon she'd clear it out. Charlotte hated clutter of any kind. Like Arthur, she believed in periodic pruning. Whether Jake would be pruned was still an open question.

She went and stood by her desk.

Jake followed her into the room.

"Close the door," Charlotte said.

He did, then turned to her. He said, "I forgot about the meeting. I would have told you if I remembered."

"Tell me what's happened," she said.

Jake shrugged. "What do you mean?"

"You seem less wretched today."

Jake's eyes lit up. "I found out that Kathy has regained consciousness."

"Lucky you," Charlotte said. Her leverage over Jake had been reduced, but not eliminated. "So what's up with Liz?"

"I don't know. I haven't had a chance to talk to her. You wouldn't let me."

"Don't blame me," Charlotte said. She crossed her arms. "I want you to draft a letter to LoveBugg in my name. Perhaps secretarial work is all you're good for."

Jake's face darkened, his hands tightened. He turned away from her and took a few steps toward the corner of her room. Then he shocked her by breaking out laughing.

Is it happening? Charlotte wondered. *Is he falling apart?*

"Well?" she said.

"I've just realised something."

"What's that?"

"If I don't take control of my life, someone else will be happy to. You or Liz or Grennan." He shook his head, then walked over to Charlotte. "Maybe it's time I decide for myself what I want to do."

Charlotte flinched as Jake stepped closer. He'd always been so predictable. Until now. He looked like he might strike her. Instead, he took Charlotte's face in his hands and kissed her. She was too surprised to pull away. His lips were softer than she would have expected. His fingers hot against her cheeks. She closed her eyes when he kissed her a second time.

Jake released her. He said, "I've wanted to do that since the first time we met."

Charlotte had too, but she didn't say so. She opened her eyes.

"What about Liz?"

Jake shook his head. "I should have ended things with her a long time ago."

There was a look in his eyes, something Charlotte saw the first time they met. A hint of the man Jake could become.

"I guess I'll go," Jake said.

"Wait."

This time, she kissed him, looping her arms around his neck and pulling his lips down to hers. She pulled away after a moment.

"I wanted this too," Charlotte said.

The door opened.

Liz stood in the doorway. Her eyes were wild. A furious howl ripped out of her mouth. She grabbed a book from Charlotte's shelf and threw it. Charlotte ducked as the book flew over her head.

"Slut," Liz screamed, then turned on her heel and stalked out of the room.

"Liz," Jake said.

Charlotte held his arm. "Let her go."

"I have to go after her. She's upset."

"Let her be upset," Charlotte said. "It's not going to kill her."

CHAPTER TWENTY-ONE

Liz fumed as her Honda sped down the road. She felt like driving into someone. Mowing down people on the footpath.

That evil slut.

She couldn't believe Charlotte had bewitched Jake. Her man. But men were weak, even the best of them, and Charlotte must have tricked him. Liz would wipe the smug smile off her face.

But first she needed to take care of something else.

Colin.

Lying dead in his apartment with a dishcloth down his throat. She had to destroy the evidence.

Liz stopped at a petrol station, where she filled a jerrycan with petrol. It would be obvious that it was arson, once the forensics people determined that petrol was involved, but so what? A good fire would destroy the evidence of her visit.

Colin had been a nasty piece of work and Liz was sure he had enemies. Who could predict where a murder investigation would lead?

Speaking of nasty pieces of work, Liz was going to make Charlotte pay for trying to steal Jake.

Tears rolled down Liz's cheek, blurring her vision. She'd never wipe that awful image from her mind. Jake and Charlotte standing in the middle of Charlotte's office, holding each other, kissing tenderly.

"Bitch," Liz screamed.

Her voice bounced around inside the car.

She reached her apartment building, grabbed the jerrycan of petrol, and hurried up to Colin's apartment. Many of their neighbours were away, visiting family over the Christmas break. She was relieved she met no one.

Colin lay in the kitchen where she'd left him. His face had lost its colour. Out of curiosity she touched his body and found it stiff and cold. Corpses were fascinating. Liz would have liked to observe what happened to Colin's body over the coming days, but she thought it was better to tidy things up here sooner rather than later.

She poured half the petrol over his head, and splashed the rest around the apartment, especially on the couch where she had sat the previous night.

Once she was satisfied, Liz threw a lit match on the floor in the kitchen, and another one in the sitting room.

The carpet caught fire with a fantastic *whoosh*.

When the fire was burning nicely, she stepped out into the corridor and closed the door behind her.

A man was approaching her from the end of the corridor. Vaguely familiar-looking. One of the men from last night. Colin's friend. Liz watched him, saw him look at her, his eyes tracking down to the jerrycan in her hand.

Liz turned and walked the other way, towards the fire escape. She forced herself to move slowly, calmly. To not look back until she was already at the end of the corridor. Then she couldn't resist. The man had just reached Colin's door. He was looking at it with his head cocked, and a puzzled expression.

Listening.

He didn't realise it was the fire he could hear. The man looked down, at the crack under the door, as the first wisps of smoke snaked out.

His eyes darted back to Liz.

Now he understood.

"Shit," Liz muttered.

She pushed through the fire door and ran down the stairs.

CHAPTER TWENTY-TWO

On the top floor, Jake made his way down the fluorescent-lit corridor to Arthur Grennan's office. He was giddy with excitement after what had happened in Charlotte's office. He'd surprised himself by kissing her, but the bigger surprise was that she had reciprocated.

He felt awful that Liz had seen them, but he would have had to break the news to her some time.

There was another difficult conversation he needed to have. Charlotte had said he was being paid less than other associates, despite all his years in the company. It sounded like Mr. Grennan didn't value him. Jake was now so far outside his comfort zone, he decided he might as well keep pushing.

Una Atkins, Mr. Grennan's secretary, was at her desk outside Grennan's office. She looked up when Jake approached. Una was so frosty, she always reminded Jake of a disapproving teacher he'd had when he was a kid. She was probably only ten years older than Jake, but she had one of those faces that belongs to a different era.

"I'd like to see Mr. Grennan."

Una reached for her diary.

"When?"

"Now."

A supercilious smile washed over her face.

"Mr. Grennan is not available today. I think he has an opening in the second week of January if that would suit you?"

Normally Jake would have turned and gone away, tail between his legs. Not now. He walked past Una, opened the door to Grennan's office and stepped inside.

The office was huge, stretching far to the left and right and enjoying spectacular views over the canal basin and surrounding area. It smelled like leather and aftershave.

The lighting here was more subdued than in the rest of the building. A large desk sat near the window. On the left side of the room, a cluster of three huge leather couches were grouped around a glass coffee table.

Mr. Grennan was perched on one couch, talking to Dermot Blake, the CEO of Ireland's largest bank. Blake's face was familiar from news reports, where he constantly seemed to be in trouble. He was almost as old as Grennan, but his thin grey hair was set in a fresher style than Grennan's and his face wasn't so stern.

All the same, Jake felt a sudden revulsion at the two men, sitting there like a couple of vampires, in their dark suits. Grennan gave Jake a cold look.

"What's this?"

"I'm sorry, Mr. Grennan," Una said. She nodded so deep it was almost a bow, and tugged Jake's arm. "I told him you were in a meeting."

"I want to talk about my salary," Jake said. Una's grip was like a vice. He turned to her. "Get your fucking hand off me or I'll sue the arse off you."

Dermot Blake broke out laughing. "He sounds like one of my traders, Arthur."

"I do apologise," Grennan said.

"You should be apologising to me," Jake said. He started walking towards the two men. "You waste years of my life, expect me to work every second of the day, pass me over for promotion again and again, and my salary is still…"

Jake paused. He was hyperventilating with excitement, and he had trouble finishing the sentence.

Arthur Grennan's scowl deepened. "I am having a discussion with Mr. Blake. Leave."

"You're having a discussion with me now."

Dermot Blake sat back in his chair, appearing genuinely amused.

Grennan shook his head. "Still what?" he said. "Your salary is still what?"

"Inadequate. I gave this company everything."

"Mr. Whelan, we don't want *everything*. We want results."

Jake shook his head. "I demand a better package."

"I'm not open to demands. If you don't find our compensation package satisfactory, you may go elsewhere. Goodbye."

"Come on," hissed Una, almost in Jake's ear.

"That's it?" Jake said. "I've worked here a decade and that's it? Then fuck you. I quit."

Even in the dim room, Jake could see Grennan's cheeks flush.

"Excuse me?"

"I'll write it up formally on a piece of toilet paper if you'd like."

Grennan got to his feet. His eyes blazed. "Mr. Whelan, how dare you?"

"I dare." Jake said, "I'd rather flip burgers than work in this kip."

"Bravo!" Dermot Blake clapped his hands together excitedly. He glanced at Grennan. "Sorry, Arthur, but I love a bit of gumption."

Jake turned and walked out the door. Una was right behind him.

What did I just do?

In the space of twenty minutes he'd lost both his girlfriend and his job. His life, as he knew it, was over.

Una closed the door, then put her hands on her hips. "Well, I never thought you had a spine."

Jake tried to think of a retort, until he saw her face. An expression that almost looked like admiration.

She said, "I've never seen anyone talk to Arthur like that."

"But I failed," Jake said miserably.

The secretary shrugged. "I don't know," she said. "Did you?"

CHAPTER TWENTY-THREE

Jake made his way back to the third floor. Friday, lunchtime, the building quiet. Anyone with any sense would be out enjoying life. And now Jake would be, too. He ran his hand along the wall as he walked, and he broke out laughing.

He thought of how surprised Mr. Grennan must have felt to have a staff member burst into his private office and interrupt him like that.

No wonder Dermot Blake had been so amused.

Jake could hardly believe he'd quit, but Fergal Long, the security guard, was waiting outside his office, and that made it real.

"Sorry," Fergal said. "I don't like doing this."

Jake nodded. "Not your fault."

Fergal sighed and started to read from a sheet of paper. "I have to inform you that Grennan and Brennan and/or you have terminated your employment with the firm. You are not required to serve your notice period. In fact, you are not permitted to so do. The firm requests that you vacate the premises with immediate effect, taking only your personal belongings. The firm requests that you not speak to any other member of staff. The firm would remind you of Section 4.1.A of your employment contract—"

"I get it," Jake said.

"I have to read it all. Sorry. I know it's a bunch of legalese bullshit. No offence."

"None taken." Jake said, "I'll pack up while you finish."

He went into his office and got his coat, emptied his personal things out of the drawer in his desk and stuffed them in the pockets of his coat. Hoping he wasn't forgetting anything, he made his way over to his desktop, so he could shut it down.

"Whoa, whoa, whoa," Fergal said. "They uh, they don't want you to access the firm's computer systems."

"Of course."

Jake stepped out of the room and turned to go to Charlotte's office. He needed to talk to her. Fergal blocked his path. He flashed an apologetic smile.

"Like I say, I really hate doing this. But I can't let you talk to other members of staff."

Jake didn't say anything this time. Shaking his head, he walked down the corridor. Fergal limped along behind him. The few people who were around watched as Jake was marched out of the building.

Fergal and Jake stood side by side, as the elevator carried them down.

"At times like this, I think of Seneca," Fergal said. "He said, 'Every new beginning comes from some other beginning's end.' Isn't that beautiful?"

Jake didn't answer. All he could think was that he wanted to see Charlotte.

When the door opened, they stepped out onto the deserted lobby. The reception desk was unmanned.

"Where's Liz?"

"Don't know," Fergal said. He held out his hand. Jake shook it. "Anyway, all the best, Jake."

"You too."

Jake stepped outside into the freezing December air. He started walking in the direction of the hospital. It might take him half an hour to walk there, maybe forty minutes, but he didn't mind.

In fact, he breathed easier with every step.

The anger he'd felt at Grennan began to ease. Maybe the old bastard wasn't so bad. Maybe he was actually right. No one had forced Jake to work there. If he didn't like it, he could have left years ago.

A car horn sounded nearby. Jake looked around to see a gleaming Jaguar pulled in at the side of the road.

Jake leaned down to peer in the front passenger window as it powered down.

"Well?" asked Charlotte.

"I quit," he said. "I told Grennan I'd rather flip burgers."

She smiled. "Get in."

Jake sat into the passenger seat. The car's interior was warm and smelled like vanilla. The news was on the radio, the volume low.

"How do you feel?" Charlotte said.

"Good question." Jake took stock of himself. "I feel… great. I was heading for the hospital. I wanted to tell Kathy the truth about what happened." Jake took a breath and let it out. "No more secrets. No more excuses."

"I'll go with you."

Charlotte launched the Jaguar back into traffic. She started to say something but Jake shushed her. An item on the news had caught his attention. A fire at an apartment building.

"Could you turn the volume up?" he said.

Charlotte tapped a button on the steering wheel and the radio got louder.

"Oh my god." Jake felt the colour draining from his face.

"What?" Charlotte said.

"Did you hear that?"

"Something about a fire?"

Jake said, "That's where Liz lives."

CHAPTER TWENTY-FOUR

Charlotte's eyes widened with understanding. A fire in Liz's building could be no coincidence. What had she done?

Jake hoped she hadn't hurt herself. If she did, it was on him.

"I need to find out what's happening," Jake said.

Charlotte changed direction at once.

They didn't talk. Jake couldn't have spoken even if he'd wanted to.

As the building came into view, he saw dozens of people standing around. The fire brigade had blocked the road off.

As soon as the car stopped, Jake flung open the door and hurried to the line of people standing looking up at one of the apartment blocks. Smoke billowed out of a cracked window on the floor above Liz's apartment.

Thank god.

It wasn't Liz.

The lady next to Jake was eighty years old if she was a day, and was dressed up like she was going out to the opera.

"Have you heard what happened?" Jake asked her.

"They haven't told us anything. It's probably a chip pan. Those things are lethal. Ooh, look at that."

Paramedics emerged from the lobby, carrying a body-bag on a stretcher.

Jake ran over to them.

"Is it a woman?" he asked.

"Out of the way," a fireman shouted.

"Man or woman?" Jake shouted back.

"A man. Now move back."

"Is anyone else hurt?"

The fireman shook his head as he hurried to the ambulance. Jake watched it go. He made his way back to the car, sat down in the passenger seat.

"It's not Liz."

Charlotte said nothing, just stared at the smoke billowing out of the building. Jake knew what she was thinking. It was still a hell of a coincidence.

"I should call her." Jake pulled out his phone. He dialled Liz's number and waited impatiently for her to answer.

Finally, Liz picked up.

"Are you okay?" Jake said. "I'm outside your building. I heard about the fire."

Liz said, "I can't believe you let that bitch… Anyway, never mind. Jake, I want you to answer a question truthfully. Do you love me?"

"Liz… I… this isn't the time for a relationship talk."

A long pause.

"Okay," she said. "We can talk later. Once I clean up this mess."

"What mess?"

"You know. All this stuff. Don't worry. I'll wipe the slate. Are you okay with using a different name?"

"What?"

"It's no big deal. After a week, you forget the old stuff anyway."

"What are you talking about? Where are you?"

"I'll call you later."

With that, Liz ended the call.

Charlotte looked at Jake. "What did she say?"

"I don't know what she was going on about. Something about starting a new life, and wiping the slate. Whether I'm okay with a new name."

"Jake, it sounds like she's in a dangerous frame of mind."

"You might be right. She wouldn't tell me where she is." Jake's stomach churned with fear. He had an idea. "Maybe her father can help. I mean, he can't speak, but he has an aide."

Charlotte shrugged. "I guess it's worth a try."

He brought up Google on his phone and looked up Grüne Felder, the Munich hospital where Liz's father was being cared for.

He found a number and called it. A man picked up after two rings.

"Hallo? Womit kann ich Ihnen behilflich sein?"

"I'm sorry. Do you speak English?"

"Yes. How can I help?"

"I'd like to speak to the aide who cares for Mr. Dubois, please. Mr. Christian Dubois."

"We don't have a resident by that name."

Jake felt a stab of irritation.

"You must know him. A French gentleman. He's paralysed. He has a daughter here in Ireland who video calls him every week."

"We have no French patients at all. Perhaps you have the wrong number."

"Is there another facility called Grüne Felder nearby? A second branch?"

"No, we only have one location. Hello? Are you still there?"

The phone fell out of Jake's hand.

Liz had lied to him.

Charlotte said, "What is it?"

"Her father is fictional. I think we need to get to the hospital. Fast."

Charlotte pulled away from the kerb with a screech.

CHAPTER TWENTY-FIVE

The supermarket across the road from St. Vincent's Hospital was always busy, but especially so at lunchtime. A lot of people were grabbing sandwiches to go, or taking the opportunity to do their grocery shopping during lunch hour.

Liz thought the self-service checkouts were her best bet.

She joined the queue, telling herself to be patient. Urgent as her business was, she couldn't afford to draw attention to herself.

Colin's friend had chased her down the corridor, and halfway down the stairs before giving up. If he hadn't seen her outside Colin's apartment as the fire started, she would have been fine. But he had to come along at exactly the wrong time. He must have been the one who called the fire brigade.

Liz had got away from there before they arrived, and had headed here to pick up a few things.

She tapped the back of the steak knife against her palm, irritated by the feel of the plastic cover. She wanted to rip it off.

In her other hand, she held a new meat tenderiser. The one she'd used on Colin had been so effective. It was a pity she hadn't brought it with her, but she'd forgotten. No harm, anyway. She'd found a new one easy enough, and she liked its heft.

Liz shuffled forwards, following those ahead of her as they moved gradually closer to the checkouts.

She really liked Jake.

She hoped he'd come around to her way of thinking. Starting over was easy, but Liz didn't want to do it alone. Her heart was set on Jake.

Only Jake.

No one was going to get in the way.

She got to the checkout and paid for her purchases.

Time for a visit to the hospital. Liz was going to make things easy for Jake and one day he would thank her.

CHAPTER TWENTY-SIX

Jake ran inside the hospital. He'd left Charlotte to park the car. There was no time to waste, if his fears were warranted. In the corridor, he ran into the nurse named Shilpa.

"Is Dr. O'Brien still here?"

"Yes, but—"

"Where? What ward?"

Shilpa pointed.

Jake didn't stop, couldn't stop.

He ran past the nurse and burst into the room.

It was a private room and Kathy was sitting up in her bed, supported by multiple cushions. The bedside table was covered with bouquets of flowers. A middle-aged man in a suit sat next to the bed with a notebook. He was taking notes while she talked. Jake let out a breath he hadn't realised he was holding.

"Kathy?"

"Jake? What are you doing here?"

He walked over and stopped beside her bed. "I'm so glad you're alright."

She smiled weakly before gesturing to the man at her side.

"This is Detective Tom Ryan," she said. "He's asking me about what happened."

Jake nodded a greeting to the plainclothes officer.

"Do you remember?" Jake asked.

Kathy frowned. "I was at home. I remember getting a call, but then… I'm not sure…"

"It was me," Jake said. "I called."

"Yes, seeing you reminds me."

The detective gave Jake a sharp look.

"What was it about?" Kathy asked.

Charlotte appeared in the doorway. She walked over, stopping a short distance from the bed.

Jake took a breath. He knew he would feel better once he had got the truth off his chest.

"I needed your help. I'd just been passed over for promotion at work."

Kathy gazed at him, her face blank. "I don't remember. They say it might take a while for my memory to return."

"You and I met in a café to talk. Then we walked outside. You got on your bike. That was when you got hit by the car. I was there. I saw it."

The detective leaned forward. His voice was low, gruff. "Why didn't you report this?"

"My girlfriend was the one who was driving." Jake glanced at Charlotte. "My ex-girlfriend."

"Her?" the detective said.

"No. The driver's name is Liz Dubois. She said Kathy was dead. She said we had to get out of there. I'm sorry I listened to her. I was an idiot."

Ryan said, "So that's who we saw on the CCTV. We have a team looking for that car."

Kathy touched the detective's wrist. "I'm sure it was an accident. Please don't be angry at Jake. I'm starting to remember." She closed her eyes for a moment. "I dropped something. Right? Then a car came out of nowhere."

"Yes," Jake said. "Only I'm starting to think it wasn't an accident. I've discovered that Liz has been lying to me. I'm not sure what's going on, but there's a fire in her apartment building."

Ryan cocked an eyebrow. "Now?"

"Yes. Maybe Liz wanted to knock down Kathy. I think she's dangerous. Her jealousy might be worse than I thought."

"People don't do hit-and-runs out of jealousy," Detective Ryan said. "Have you got any evidence of all this?"

"No. I'm worried Liz might be coming here. She was talking strangely. I think you need to protect Dr. O'Brien."

The detective stood up. He said, "You and I need to go down to the station. I want to take a statement from you."

"Sure," Jake said. "But you can't leave Kathy alone."

Her eyes widened. "Am I really in danger?"

"Don't worry," the detective said. "You're safe as can be."

The lights overhead flickered and died. Some kind of power outage? Jake met Charlotte's gaze and saw his fear reflected in her eyes. Kathy was far from safe.

Liz was already there.

CHAPTER TWENTY-SEVEN

The room was dark for a few moments before the backup generator kicked in. Its light was hardly strong enough to chase away the gloom of the winter afternoon.

"Never seen that before," the detective said, looking around.

Jake said, "There's more I need to tell you."

"Let me check with the hospital staff first. Check that everything is alright."

Jake saw Shilpa pass the doorway.

"I have a feeling everything is not alright," he said.

Ryan turned to Jake, the movement revealing the bulge of a handgun at his hip. He covered it again with his suit jacket. "What do you mean?"

"My girlfriend, my ex-girlfriend, I think she's dangerous. That fire—"

Ryan held up a hand. "Take a breath. You're talking about the woman who was driving the car when the accident happened?"

"Yes, but I'm sure it wasn't an accident."

Kathy sat up a little straighter in bed. "She hit me deliberately?"

"And I think she's here now. She wants to harm you."

"How do you know that?" the detective asked.

"I can't be sure," Jake said. "But I talked to her on the phone, and she sounded strange."

"I'm going to be right back," the detective said. His voice was low and stern. "And you and I are going to have a long talk about this. Down at the station."

"Okay," Jake said. "But please arrange for someone to come here to guard Kathy."

Ryan stalked out the door.

Charlotte said, "He thinks you're crazy."

"Maybe." Jake looked at Kathy. A cannula in the back of her hand hooked her into an IV bag of fluids at the side of the bed. "We're going to have to move you."

Kathy said, "Jake, are you sure?"

"If Liz finds you, I don't know what she'll do."

But he did know.

Murder her, Jake thought. *That's what Liz will do.*

"Let's hurry," Charlotte said.

"Take care of the IV bag."

Charlotte grabbed the metal stand while Jake pulled the bed away from the wall. He pushed it to the door, Charlotte keeping pace, and watching the IV line.

They moved out into the dim corridor. Jake saw Ryan's silhouette down the hall. The detective was talking on his mobile, paying no attention. Jake pushed the bed the other direction. They turned the next corner, down the hall to another ward.

Jake stopped in the doorway and looked inside. There were six patients in six beds. No nurses, no doctors. He nodded to Charlotte and they wheeled the bed inside. They pushed it to the far side of the room.

"I'll be back for you soon," Jake said. "You'll be safe here."

He patted her hand, alarmed to see that she was on the brink of tears. "It'll be okay," he promised.

He and Charlotte walked back the way they had come. When they reached the door of Kathy's previous ward, Jake stopped.

The detective lay on the floor. The handle of a knife stuck out of his belly and a meat tenderiser lay on the floor next to his head. Jake crouched down, and searched in vain for a pulse.

"Come in."

Liz was standing in the middle of the room, holding the detective's pistol.

CHAPTER TWENTY-EIGHT

Liz had a crazed look in her eye, and the gun in her hand did nothing to dispel that impression. Jake looked at the dead detective at his feet and then up at his girlfriend of a year. She stood about four metres away in the dim light of the backup generator.

"Where is she?" Liz said. "Where's Dr. O'Brien?"

"Doesn't matter," Jake said. "It's over."

"This place is over, this life. But we can start again. We can go somewhere new, *be* someone new."

"You killed a man."

A confused expression passed over Liz's face. "You mean him?" Liz used the gun to point at Ryan's body. "He got in our way. Everything I've done, I've done for us."

"I called your father's hospital. They've never heard of him."

"Sorry for fibbing. It was just a white lie. I had to make you stay with me. I needed time to show you we belong together."

"You lied about everything. The hit-and-run wasn't an accident, was it?"

Liz said, "I didn't plan it."

"How can you say we belong together?" Jake asked. "With no honesty, with no trust, with no love?"

"Of course, I love you," Liz said. That's why I'm doing this."

"And you'll even cut out the power in a hospital, even burn down an apartment building, to get what you want?"

Liz raised the gun and pointed it at Jake's chest. "We don't have time to debate it. Trust me, Jake. We'll start a new life together. Tell me where Dr. O'Brien is so we can be on our way."

The old Jake would have stood aside, told her where Kathy was and hoped for the best. But something had happened to Jake in the last twenty-four hours. He glanced at Charlotte. Only the tightness in her eyes betrayed her concern. Then he looked back at Liz.

"No," Jake said.

He took a step forward.

"Don't do anything stupid," Liz said, aiming the gun at his head.

Jake said, "All I've done is stupid things. But not anymore."

He took another step.

"Stop. I'll shoot."

"I thought you loved me."

"If you force me to shoot you, I'll do it."

Jake smiled. Despite the ferocious pounding of his heart, he suddenly felt free.

"Do what you want. I'll do what's right for me."

Liz gripped the pistol with two hands, steadying it.

Jake took another step closer.

He was almost within reach now. Was Liz willing to put a bullet in his brain? Jake had no idea. He closed more of the gap between them. Only a couple of feet separated them.

"Stop," she shouted. She swung the gun to the side, pointing it at Charlotte's head. "Stop or I'll blow that bitch's brains out."

Jake lunged forward.

He smacked the gun to the side. There was an explosion of heat and gas as the gun fired. A bullet blasted through a vase of flowers and blew a hole in the wall.

Jake shoved Liz backwards.

She tried to raise the gun, but Jake smacked it again and threw himself at her. The gun's barrel spun in the direction of the window and went off again.

Glass shattered and freezing December air rush into the room.

Liz hit Jake in the nose with the butt of the gun, knocking him to the floor. She turned the gun on him again and aimed it.

I'm going to die, Jake thought.

Then a glass vase arced through the air and hit Liz in the throat. It fell to the floor and shattered into smithereens at her feet. She gasped and dropped the gun.

Charlotte appeared next to Jake, looking like she didn't quite believe what she'd done.

Jake got to his feet.

So did Liz. They heard footsteps pounding the floor in the hall outside. Security staff, Jake hoped. There was no escape for Liz now.

She must have been thinking the same thing.

With a furious howl, she grabbed the gun off the floor and threw herself at the window, bringing her hands up to protect her face as she launched herself through the broken glass.

CHAPTER TWENTY-NINE

Dr. O'Brien's room was near the entrance to the Emergency Department, the window lying about ten feet above the ground. Liz was aware of that, as she launched herself into space, but she had no idea what exactly was beneath her.

Anyway, she had no choice. She wasn't going to let herself be arrested and put in prison.

Not again.

She fell into a row of bushes growing against the wall of the building. They were ferny and low, and did little to cushion her landing.

The impact winded her and knocked the gun out of her hand. But she scrambled to her feet and found she was alright.

She picked up the gun and looked around. There was no one about. Just sirens in the distance.

She'd done it.

She'd got away.

On her feet, she moved quickly away from the building, stopping at the edge of the footpath. She looked back and saw Jake and Charlotte looking out the window at her.

The sight of them together was enough to fill her with fresh rage.

She pointed the gun at them and squeezed the trigger once, twice, three times, until she had no bullets left. Charlotte and Jake ducked out of sight at the first shot.

Liz had no idea where the bullets went.

"You're dead," she screamed over the wail of sirens.

There was a lot to do. She had to create a new identity. She had to disappear and start again. She had to find someone new, someone who deserved her.

Before she went, she'd take her revenge on Jake and Charlotte. They weren't going to get away with this. For now, she had to run.

An ambulance shot up the road towards the Emergency Department.

"Liz," Jake shouted. "Wait."

She turned to see him leaning out the window, one arm stretched out as if he wanted to touch her. Tears of anger blurred her vision.

"It's not fair," she screamed, and stomped her foot on the ground.

"Liz!" Jake shouted again.

Distracted, she stumbled, tripped over her own feet.

She fell into the path of the ambulance.

It was moving too fast to stop, and Liz was off-balance.

She couldn't recover.

Would never recover.

The ambulance smashed into her. The last thing Liz heard was Jake's voice, still calling her name.

CHAPTER THIRTY

Two weeks later, Jake and Charlotte visited Kathy O'Brien at her home. The house was a comfortable semi-detached building, nestled in the middle of a housing estate close to the sea. Philip, Kathy's husband, gave Jake's hand a firm shake on the doorstep and led them into the kitchen.

Colourful children's drawings were stuck to the fridge. The whole family beamed out of snapshots framed on the wall.

They followed Philip through the kitchen to the conservatory, where Kathy sat in a padded futon, reading a Harlan Coben novel.

She looked up when they came in, and gave Jake a brilliant smile. She had been released from St. Vincent's the previous day. Jake gave her a hug and said, "You remember my girlfriend?"

It felt good to call Charlotte that, and for them to be there as a couple.

Jake had brought flowers. Charlotte, a get-well-soon card.

"Sit down," Kathy said.

Jake watched Philip as he took the flowers and went off to make tea.

"I thought your husband might take a swing at me," Jake whispered.

"Don't be silly. Philip doesn't blame you. Neither do I. You know that. By the way, I had another talk with the new detective, Thompson."

Jake nodded. Thompson was Ryan's replacement. Jake had met him at Ryan's funeral and spoken to him on two other occasions. He seemed like a decent man, though Jake couldn't say he'd enjoyed their talks together.

"We've spoken," Jake said.

"I reminded him that I bear you no hard feelings. I also reminded him of the stress you were under at the time of the incident and how you saved my life in the hospital. I hope they won't cause you too much trouble."

Charlotte squeezed Jake's hand.

"Even if they try," Charlotte said, "I'll make sure nothing comes of it."

Jake knew she meant it. She was willing to bring all her firepower to bear for him, if necessary.

Kathy pointed to a tabloid on the couch beside her.

"I don't usually read these rags, but, honestly, the things these journalists have found out about Liz…"

Jake nodded.

Liz Dubois wasn't actually her name and she had no paralysed father, no living family at all. But she had plenty of names, which Interpol was still trying to get straight. She'd been Kara Jansen while she lived in the Netherlands for three months, Bridget Bisset during eight months in Glasgow, Lisa-Anne Reich during a spring in Marseilles. A string of false IDs and violent incidents coincided with her relocations.

Jake hadn't begun to wrap his head around it.

While they chatted, Jake looked Kathy over. Every time he had visited her in hospital, she had perked up a little more, and now she almost looked normal, though a pair of crutches leaned against the side of the couch.

Brain damage had been Jake's main concern, but there was no indication that Kathy had suffered any, and, for that, Jake was grateful.

An hour passed quickly, and when the light began to fade, Jake and Charlotte excused themselves. Kathy saw them off from the doorstep. She said she needed to get up from her seat once in a while or she'd go crazy. Jake promised to visit again, some evening during the week. His new job would keep him busy during the daytime.

Jake had been surprised when Dermot Blake's secretary called him the previous week and asked him to hold for Mr. Blake. Jake had been even more surprised when the banker came on the line and offered him a position at the bank.

He'd accepted, though the position in the compliance department wasn't his ideal job. He'd have preferred to be a park ranger. But Blake had promised him he'd be dealing with land the bank had bought, so in any case there was a tenuous connection to the earth. Jake figured the work would be a change anyway, and a change was a step in the right direction. At least he'd have an income while he figured out what he really wanted to do. This time, the decision would be his. No one would make it for him.

As Jake and Charlotte walked down Kathy's driveway, Charlotte leaned in and kissed Jake on the cheek.

She said, "I want you all to myself for the weekend."

"You got it. Let's grab a pizza and catch up on Netflix. It can be a nice pizza, by the way. You've got that bonus to spend."

He was referring to the one Charlotte had received for her work on the LoveBugg deal. It had already made Grennan and Brennan a fortune.

"I'm not paying," Charlotte said. "Don't forget you owe me ten thousand."

Jake laughed.

"I thought you forgot about the bet."

"I never forget. Sometimes I forgive."

As they walked the rest of the way to the Jaguar, Jake realised that the old, familiar tightness in his chest hadn't bothered him for days, maybe a week. He took an easy breath, and squeezed Charlotte's hand.

"What?" she said.

Jake shook his head, because it was nothing, except that he was happy.

Printed in Great Britain
by Amazon